# TO DATE

a *Fated Match* novel

# VICTORIA DAVIES

Entangled Publishing, LLC
2614 South Timberline Road
Suite 109
Fort Collins, CO 80525
Visit our website at www.entangledpublishing.com.

Covet is an imprint of Entangled Publishing, LLC.

Edited by Candace Havens
Cover design by Louisa Maggio
Cover art by iStock

Manufactured in the United States of America

First Edition June 2015

*For my family that put up with me constantly huddling over a keyboard while I wrote this book. I am forever grateful for your love and support.*

# Chapter One

There comes a time in every immortal's life when you wonder if the universe is screwing with you.

Today was that day.

"Not a single decent match in all of New York City?" Melissa asked in disbelief.

Abbey shook her head. "I ran the search twice. Maybe we need to expand your dating criteria?"

"You know how long I've waited to use this dating agency," she said. "And now you're telling me I'm the only vampire within the city limits who breaks your fancy matching algorithm?"

"It's not that you have no matches," Abbey tried. "Just nothing higher than the recommended 75 percent cut off."

Looked like the bad luck that had been following her for decades had struck again.

Melissa collapsed back in her chair and rubbed the bridge of her nose. Fated Match was the premier dating agency for supernaturals on the east coast. She had come to them because, like many of her kind, she was ready to settle down and find her mate, that one perfect person meant to spend eternity by her side.

Except she apparently didn't have one.

"You know the match rating is just a guideline. I can set you up with one of the lower pairings if you want. There was a nice warlock who matched you at 67 percent."

She looked across the untidy desk at her friend. Abbey had only come into her life because of her quest to use this agency. Her father had been skeptical about the possibilities of matchmaking, but he'd quickly changed his tune when he'd fallen head over heels for the woman in front of her now. Who knew this little human would be able to tame her ancient sire?

Since that fateful meeting she'd seen the two of them together time and again, seen the unconditional love shining out of their eyes, and she wanted that for herself.

"My match with Lucian was in the forties," Abbey reminded her. "According to the algorithm we should never have gotten together. Sometimes you can't put all your trust in the system."

Abbey's romance may have broken all the rules, but Melissa knew she wouldn't have the same luck. Her life as a vampire had been one long list of poor decisions.

"What do you recommend?" she asked with a sigh.

"Well, we've got you on the silver package right now. Access to the internet database, personal interviews with yours truly, and three handpicked blind dates. We could up you to our gold membership. That adds five more pre-select-ed dates, an extended three years of access, and boosts your profile to the top of the search page. It'll stream more traffic toward you."

"Fine," she said, handing over her credit card. "Though I have to say, those last few 'handpicked' dates left a lot to be desired."

"I swear I thought the merman was a good candidate."

"He lived in the freaking Hudson, Abbey. How would that work?"

Her friend sighed. "He said he'd gotten his legs and was trying to build a life on land."

"For a few hours a day. He had to keep his gills wet."

"So he fudged his application. I'll do better next time. We're running a big campaign right now to bring in more members. Maybe your mate just hasn't signed up yet."

"Or maybe he's on the other side of the world."

Or maybe she just didn't have one.

"My boss is thinking about opening another office on the west coast. Once it's up and running, you'll have access to supernaturals across the entire country."

And in the meantime she'd continue on as she had these past decades, running her charities, enjoying the occasional one-night stand, and envying her friends their happy endings.

"There's got to be one man in this damned city who's worth dating."

"What about humans?" Abbey offered.

Melissa glanced at her friend. She might love her dearly but she didn't have her father's restraint. Dating a human with all that lovely warm blood would be one long exercise in resisting temptation, and she had never been big on self-denial. No, she needed an immortal that could handle her superior strength, not to mention the occasional bouts of bloodlust.

"I don't think so," she replied, not wanting to offend.

"Well, let's look at your profile preferences." Abbey's fingers flew over the keyboard of the ancient desktop computer perched on the side of her desk. Though the matchmaker had managed to nab one of the most powerful vampires in the city, she was still cooped up in a tiny office that sported only one small window and an ugly metal filing cabinet.

Melissa knew she'd get claustrophobic working in there every day, but Abbey seemed to love it. Lord knew Lucian had the money to ensure the mortal never worked another day in her life, but Abbey refused to leave. She liked having a hand in bringing people together.

*If only she could work her talents on me,* Melissa mused.

"I think we should open up your were-creature options," Abbey said, focusing on her screen. "Right now you'll only consider predatory species. I know a really nice were-mouse I could set you up with."

Melissa arched a brow. Vampires were predators by nature. She wanted similar instincts in a mate. Then again, beggars couldn't be choosers, and for the first time in her life, it seemed she'd fallen into that category.

"Fine," she said. "All weres welcome. Maybe I'll meet that one special were-squirrel that changes my opinion forever."

"Done," Abbey said with a few clicks of her mouse. "Now the only other restrictions you have are on what we call the death races."

"Vampires," she clarified. Despite her fangs, she'd never been a fan of dating her own species. When you dealt with immortals centuries old, you tended to uncover master manipulators and ancient beings whose sanity was beginning to wear. "I keep telling you, any age gap of more than a century causes issues."

Abbey leveled her with an annoyed stare. "You know your father is several hundred years older than I am."

It was true Lucian cornered the market on ancient beings in New York. Hell, he'd been old as dirt when he'd first come into her life. She still remembered looking across the tavern as a young child and seeing him prowl toward her and her mother. Though not a drop of blood related them, Lucian had been the only father she'd ever known, and when an accident had nearly killed her, he'd saved her the only way he could.

Hence her current penchant for drinking blood and avoiding the sun.

Melissa waved her hand. "Lucian doesn't count. You guys broke all the other rules anyway. Age was the least of your worries."

Shaking her head, Abbey turned back to the computer. "I know you don't like dating vamps, but there are other beings in the category. It covers demons, ghouls, phantoms, and necromancers."

"Demons are even more vicious than my people are," she said, ticking off the types on her fingers. "Ghouls tend to be messy with their food. Carcasses in bed, severed fingers in the coffee pots. Such a drag in the mornings. As for phantoms, they are literally incorporeal. I'm not quite ready to swear off sex in order to have a meaningful relationship."

"That just leaves necromancers. All the fun of a human with the durability and lifespan of an immortal."

"Abbey." The single word was a reproof.

The other woman sighed. "I know."

"I'm surprised their kind is even allowed to join Fated Match."

"I know there are issues between the necromancer and the vamp population, but that still leaves the rest of the supernatural world for them to date in. They need help finding their mates just as much as any other species."

"Certainly no member of a death race would go near them. Not with the trouble they've caused in the past, and their ability to control the dead. I'm not taking a chance on a man who could make me hop up and down on one foot with the snap of his fingers." She looked away. "Besides, you know as well as I do, Lucian has been dealing with uprisings in the necromancer community for weeks."

Abbey sighed. "It's probably just as well. With them banned from major cities, you'd be looking at a long distance relationship anyway." Her fingers tapped against the keys before she shook her head. "Sorry, but it looks like there's no way to open up your match possibilities any more than they already are."

"Perfect." She tilted her head back. Vampires spent hundreds of years alone, searching for their mates. She had barely passed her first century. Even if Abbey could find decent pairings, the odds of finding a long-term companion were slim.

"Don't give up hope. We have mixers a few times a month. I'll put you on the guest list for the next one."

"Thanks." She pushed from her seat. "We're still on for dinner Thursday with Lucian, correct?"

"We'll be there," Abbey agreed. "Lucian wants to talk to you about beefing up security. You know he's worried about the necromancer situation."

She rolled her eyes. "I'm not having bodyguards tail my every move. I work on several human charities. How would I explain my new vampire shadows?"

"You're Lucian's heir," Abbey pointed out. "Not to mention you're always in the spotlight. I saw you on the cover of the *Magical Times* last month. If the necromancers were serious about striking out at the vamp community, you'd be a good target."

Melissa opened her mouth, letting her fangs lengthen. "They may have their freaky abilities, but I'm not exactly powerless."

"Just be careful is all I'm saying."

She smiled, retracting her fangs. "I know. Don't worry, I'll hash it out with Lucian."

"Great and I'll keep working on your matches. Promise."

With a last wave, she left the small office.

Melissa walked down the white hallway into the reception room of Fated Match. Outside the glass double doors lay a bustling Manhattan street. Night had fallen long ago, but the street was still full of people rushing home after a long day.

Inside the business was a tastefully decorated waiting room. Several pink chairs lined the walls, and two women waited for their appointments. Unlike a human establishment, the coffee table in the center of the room was littered with magazines featuring fairy supermodels and warlock doctors preaching the latest health tips for a happy immortality.

Melissa could try all the touted new herbs, but she knew the truth. A happy immortality required finding her mate —

that one person born to spend lifetimes by her side.

"How'd it go, Melissa?"

She glanced at the white reception desk to see a familiar face.

"Chloe," she greeted, walking over to the witch. "I haven't seen you in a while."

"Just got back from a vacation. The Bermuda Triangle is lovely this time of year."

Melissa eyed the other woman's tan enviously. Sun hadn't touched her pale skin in over a hundred years.

"Has Abbey set you up with anyone decent?" Chloe asked.

She shook her head. "Striking out so far."

"Well, don't despair. We're getting walk-ins all the time."

As if conjured by her words, the bell over the door chimed.

Melissa turned to see the new arrival and stopped cold. The sight would have robbed her of breath if she'd had working lungs.

The most beautiful man she'd ever seen stepped through the glass doors.

He was tall enough to make her feel small, and given that she approached six feet, that was no simple task. Though he moved with grace, he had the body of a warrior, all fit and toned. His navy suit jacket was slung over one arm, and the light blue dress shirt underneath had been rolled up to show off his forearms. Melissa eyed the golden skin as she fought to keep from licking her lips.

Her eyes raked over his broad chest before rising to his face. His square jaw was firm, his patrician nose perfect. Eyelashes any woman would envy shaded his bright blue gaze as auburn hair tumbled around his face. It was slightly too long, as if he'd put off getting it cut, but her fingers itched to run through the soft waves.

As handsome as he was, however, it was the magic rolling off him that most drew Melissa. Power pulsed from him, raising the hairs on her arms.

The man glanced around the office, his gaze sweeping over the two women in the waiting room, who were eyeing him just as hungrily as Melissa was. Finally those icy blue eyes landed on her, and electricity sizzled through her body.

He strode forward without ever taking his gaze from her.

Her fangs ached in her gums. Desire shot through her to pool low in her abdomen. Rarely did she ever react so quickly to a possible partner, but for this man she'd make an exception. Hell, she'd kick Abbey out of her office and do him on the desk if he'd let her.

"Welcome to Fated Match," Chloe said, slightly breathless herself. "Pairing mates together since 1704."

Those intense eyes flicked away from her, and Melissa mourned the loss.

"I'm interested in your services," he said to Chloe.

Melissa bit back a moan as she let the deep, velvety voice roll over her. He had the sort of voice that made women think of wicked acts in tangled sheets.

"Have you ever registered with us before?" Chloe asked.

"First time." He turned to her and held out a hand. "Tarian Drake. Pleasure to meet you."

"Melissa Redgrave," she replied, sliding her hand into his.

Magic snapped at her fingertips as he wrapped his hand

around hers. A shiver of awareness ran down her spine. Had she ever lusted for someone this fast before? She couldn't remember.

"Are you a member, Ms. Redgrave?"

"Melissa, please," she breathed. "And yes."

His smile lent a boyishness to his face that was oddly endearing. "Good."

Taking her hand back, she cleared her throat and glanced at Chloe. "Abbey's free."

"So is Vivian," she replied, pressing a call button. "Mr. Drake, my boss will be out in a moment to handle your intake interview. She'll be able to field all your questions about our offerings here at Fated Match."

"Thank you for your assistance." His gaze flicked back to her. "Would you recommend the services here, Melissa?"

The sound of her name on his lips lit the blood in her veins on fire.

"They have an excellent reputation," she replied. "It's definitely worth your time if you're serious about finding a mate."

"Very," he said. "This agency was recommended by a friend who had success here."

"They have a high match rate," she agreed.

"Yes, I remember reading a story about your father finding his mate here, did he not?"

She arched a brow. "You recognized me?"

"Few in our world would not."

"Then you have me at a disadvantage, I'm afraid. I'll have to learn more about you."

Another grin curved his lips. "I'm sure that can be arranged."

A click of heels in the hall signaled the arrival of the grand architect of the agency. Vivian rounded the corner in all her siren glory. For the first time, Melissa felt a twinge of jealousy when looking at the other woman. She was all generous curves and long platinum hair. Her very nature was to seduce and bewitch, and Vivian was a master of all the tricks.

"Hello there," she purred, stepping forward. "Welcome to Fated Match. I'm free to see you now if you'd like to start the registration process."

"Excellent," Tarian said. Looking back at her, he inclined his head. "It was very nice to meet you."

"And you." Her fingers found her business card automatically, and she held it out. "In case you decide not to join," she said.

He pocketed the card with a smile. "I promise to use it."

With a last look, he turned to follow Vivian down the white hallway.

She and Chloe both craned their necks for a last glimpse of him until they heard Vivian's door click closed.

"Good god," Chloe exhaled.

"You had better tell Abbey I want the full scoop the moment he's registered."

"Get in line, honey," she replied. "That man is going to be in high demand."

And with her luck, she'd probably get a low match rating with him.

"What do you think he is?" Chloe mused.

Melissa shook her head. "No idea but he had a pulse."

"And magic. Not a witch, though. I would have felt the connection."

"A were?"

Chloe shrugged. "Maybe, but not a wolf. They have a far more primal energy to them."

"Well, if he signs up we'll know soon enough." She rapped her knuckles on the counter. "Remember, tell Abbey I'll be expecting her call."

The witch tossed her a grin. "It pays to have inside access, eh?"

"Fingers crossed."

Melissa left the office with a smile on her face. Whatever the hell Tarian was, she sure hoped he'd be hers.

Even if only for a night.

# Chapter Two

A buzzing vibrated from her purse. Fishing out her phone, she saw Abbey's number on the screen.

"I expected your call last night," she said in greeting.

Abbey chuckled. "I know. Tarian's intake took a bit of time, and I didn't think there was any point calling during the day while you slept."

"Fair point."

"Are you at the office?"

"Yeah." Her fingers flew over her the keyboard on her laptop. "I've got the website up."

"Search him."

It barely took a minute before she was staring into the icy blue gaze of his profile picture. Finding the large red match button at the top of the page, she clicked it. The damn color pinwheel spun while she waited for the page to reload.

"Do you see it?"

"Just a sec," she replied as the page refreshed.

"A 90 percent match," Abbey said evenly, and the new page came up on Melissa's computer.

She blinked at the screen. Fated Match advised only contacting members with a match rating of 75 percent or higher. Ninety was as excellent as it was rare.

"That's amazing," she breathed.

"I know," Abbey replied. "And since you just purchased five more handpicked dates, I can guarantee you'll be at the top of his match list."

"Excellent news," she said. "Set it up, and I'm there."

She scrolled through his profile, skimming the information present. One section, however, was curiously blank.

"Uh, Abbey?" she asked. "What species is he?"

There was a pause. "Well, that's the thing. He didn't want to disclose his age or race."

"What?" She hadn't even been aware that was an option.

"Yeah, we tried, trust me, but he was pretty firm. Said he wanted to meet people who were interested in him and not his bloodline."

"But…" Some of her joy drained away. "That's a red flag, no?"

"Your call," Abbey said. "He seemed nice enough to me."

She tapped her foot. On the one hand, she really didn't have many restrictions on who she'd date. On the other, the few she had were important.

"What are they odds that he's one of the death races?"

"Slim, I'd say. He was pretty tanned for a vamp, and you touched him, right? Not a phantom."

"Right," she agreed. "I'm being silly. He could be a dancing bear, and a 90 percent rating would still warrant a meeting."

"Good girl. Okay, let me run this through the proper channels, and I'll try to set something up."

"Great. Thanks, Abbey."

"No problemo. Ciao."

After ending the call, she dropped the cell back into her purse.

She lounged back in her chair as she scrolled through the profile. Most of his information was pretty basic. His occupation was listed as something in the financial world. He'd recently moved to the city, and he was allergic to shellfish. Nothing about him screamed serial killer. She was probably fine.

"As long as you're not a demon," she said, minimizing the screen. Or a necromancer. She nearly laughed at the thought.

Pushing from her seat, she crossed her spacious office to gaze out the large windows that lined the walls. Outside, the city glittered with a million artificial lights. How times had changed.

In the reflection of the window she saw her sleek, minimalistic office. Lucian had given her this small corner of the Redgrave Foundation building years ago to help her better manage her various organizations and responsibilities. Though she spent most of her nights in this room, it was anything but warm. Like most vampires, she kept her space free of personal mementoes. While she did have a few black-and-white pictures of her mother, they stayed in a keepsake box beneath her bed rather than on display. Vampires jealously guarded their pasts, especially the stories of their transformation. Information like that could expose a weakness, and that's one thing her kind could not abide.

"Ms. Redgrave?"

She turned to see her administrative assistant poking her head through the glass door.

"Your eleven o'clock is here about the children's aid fundraiser."

"Show her in, Mary," she replied, moving back toward her desk. Most of her nights were filled with such meetings. The reps for supernatural charities had no problem working with her late hours, and many of the human ones had grown accustomed to humoring her. With the money the Redgrave family donated, they'd meet her anywhere, anytime.

"Ms. Sherman," she greeted her appointment as she strolled in. "Please be seated."

Wondering about the mysterious Tarian Drake would have to wait. Tonight she had more pressing matters to attend to.

• • •

"Well, you people move fast, I'll say that for you."

A young, female voice chuckled into the phone. "Your profile has been extremely popular, Mr. Drake. However, since you've already met Ms. Redgrave in passing, I thought I'd offer to match you two up for your first assigned date."

Tarian twirled his pen around his fingers, thinking of the tasty vampire.

Like most of her kind, she was stunning. It wasn't a matter of the race turning only attractive mortals but rather an outcome of the lifestyle. Having been hidden from the sun for years, Melissa's hair had darkened into a blood red he found oddly fascinating. Her skin was perfect alabaster, with not a single freckle to be found. Her body had been slender and lithe, also a side effect of her nature. Without a diet of high fat and sugary foods, vampires tended to lose weight in the months after their transformations and had no way of putting it back on. While he preferred his women with more curves, he couldn't fault her for something beyond her control.

But it was those eyes, those piercing emerald-green eyes that had radiated intelligence and lust that had haunted his dreams last night.

"Yes," he said. "I'd be inclined to see her."

"Excellent." The matchmaker sounded downright gleeful. "Would Friday work?"

"It should."

"As a new member, I'll expect you at seven-thirty to go over the rules of a Fated Match pairing. A car will take you to Celeste's for your eight o'clock date."

"I look forward to it," he said, jotting down the appointment. "See you then."

Disconnecting, he let out a sigh.

This could get very tricky, very fast.

"Tarian?" a voice called from beyond his door.

"Come in," he said.

The wooden door opened, and his sister stepped into the study. "I heard you talking," she said as she crossed the carpeted floor to his side. Dropping into the armchair that matched his, she curled her legs under her and gazed at the old fireplace.

"Isn't it a little warm for a fire?" she asked.

It was, but Tarian enjoyed firelight rather than the harsh

fluorescents that were so popular nowadays. "What can I do for you, Eilin?"

"The rumors are growing," she replied, her voice subdued. "People are calling for sides to be chosen."

Tarian rubbed a hand down his face. "We stay out of it as we always have. The last place we want to be is caught between the vampires and our kin."

She wrapped her arms around her knees, resting her chin on top of them like she'd done as a child so many years ago.

A soft smile curved his lips as he gazed at his sister. No matter how many decades they lived, to him she'd always be the chubby little blonde baby that had followed him around all day, every day.

"Are they wrong?" she whispered finally, staring into the fire. "The vampires have pushed us to the edge of society for centuries. If we want a real life, isn't it worth fighting for?"

"We have a real life."

She shot him a glare. "If we keep what we are secret. We have to pretend to be human half the time."

"It's better than the alternative."

"Is it?" She pushed to her feet. "Grandfather says—"

"You're too young to remember the wars," he cut her off, rising. "The vampires are an ancient and powerful faction. Add to that the fact that these are modern times, equipped with social media, camera phones, and zero anonymity. Taking them on now might risk exposing the supernatural world to the humans."

Eilin threaded her fingers through her ringlets. "How can you not hate them?"

Melissa's face flashed across his mind, and he glanced away from his sister. "Once I hated them, for longer than you've been alive," he replied. "And you know what good came out of it?"

She shook her head.

"Death. That's all. Nothing changed. It never does." He ran a hand through his hair. "So what is the use of hate?"

"You need to take a stand," she charged. "Nothing will ever change if we don't try. We have to make the ruling vampires listen to us."

"And how do you suppose we do that?" Tarian said, not bothering to hide his amusement.

This time she didn't answer.

"Eilin?"

"I don't know," she replied. "But grandfather has a plan."

A chill went down his spine. He still remembered the screams of the dying the last time they faced off against the vampires. No matter what his brethren decided, he wasn't letting Eilin get caught up in their nonsense.

"I think it'd be best if we avoid grandfather's calls for the time being," he told her. The man had never had much contact with them, but it seemed the limited time Tarian had allowed Eilin was still enough to inflict her with rebellious zeal. "There are always better solutions. Peaceful ones."

She wouldn't meet his gaze. "I'm not ashamed of what I am."

"And you think I am?"

Silence.

Anger curled through him. Casting out his hand, magic poured from his palm to flood the room. The stag head mounted on the wall above the fireplace shook its antlers as it sprang to life. It let out a guttural cry, calling for its kin.

"Grandfather is powerful," he said, his voice low. "But

so am I. I'm not ashamed of my gift, Eilin, I'm cautious."
Releasing his magic, the stag stopped moving and returned
to its original frozen position.

"Oh yeah?" she asked. "I know you joined that dating
site. Tell me, brother, what did you list as your race?"

He stiffened.

"I'm betting it wasn't necromancer," she taunted. "So
please, tell me again how proud you are of your heritage."

Knowing she'd gotten the final word, Eilin strode from
the study with her head held high.

Tarian fell back into his chair. He'd hoped New York
would be a fresh start for them. A chance to get his sister
away from the influence of their family.

But it seemed no matter where a necromancer ran, his
problems followed.

Gazing into the fire, he thought of the woman with blood-
red hair. Seeing her again was dangerous. Especially given her
last name.

*It's not worth it,* his inner voice cautioned. *There are
other women.*

Some other woman who wouldn't mean risking expulsion
from the city if she ever discovered exactly what he was.

But there was no other woman who made him burn with
a single touch. Walking into the agency, all he'd seen was her.
All he'd wanted was her. When was the last time he'd had
such a strong desire for anyone?

"It shouldn't matter what I am," he growled at the fire.
He was so much more than his death magic. Not that anyone
ever bothered to look deeper.

Even Melissa would run if she knew the truth, and he
was sick of being vilified just because of his blood. How

many chances had he walked away from? How many missed opportunities for a fulfilling life?

"Not again," he vowed. He'd come to New York for a new start and by God he'd get one. If dating a vampire wasn't a radical change, he didn't know what was.

"I'll see you Friday, Melissa," he said, saluting the flame.

For better or for worse, he was done with skulking in the shadows.

# Chapter Three

Here's hoping this date turned out better than her last three, because she could sure as hell use a pick-me-up. Melissa sat in Celeste's, staring around the elegantly decorated restaurant. Just last night she'd been in an equally stylish establishment meeting with her father and Abbey.

She'd been looking forward to the evening, since she'd seen less and less of Lucian after he'd fallen for her human friend. The prospect of a nice family dinner was one she'd been excited about.

Until Lucian had launched onto his favorite topic—new security measures. Hours that should have been spent catching up had been reallocated to an endless lecture on how she should be protecting herself. He'd even suggested she put her charitable projects on hold and leave the city for the next few weeks, until the necromancer situation was more stable.

Melissa rolled her eyes. Though she was a century old,

she'd always be his little girl. The accident that had led to her transformation had also killed her mother, a woman Lucian had loved dearly. Her mother had refused Lucian's offer to live with fangs, and her father had been unwilling to lose them both. A hundred years later and he was still doing everything he could to keep her safe, no matter how strong she'd grown in her own right.

Melissa downed the last of her water. She needed to relax. Tarian wasn't responsible for her terrible mood. She just needed to figure out a way to prove to Lucian she could take care of herself.

"A problem for another day," she said, smoothing a hand over her red dress. She'd chosen the color to complement her hair. It didn't hurt that the tight material highlighted the few curves she did possess. Not for the first time, she envied Abbey's curvaceous figure.

Though she could consume food for show, it had no effect on her body. She wasn't able to absorb any of the nutrients she needed to survive. Only blood sustained her. Luckily Celeste's was used to catering to a supernatural clientele.

Her sensitive hearing picked up an increase in the human chatter, and she glanced up.

It was easy to see what had caused the commotion.

Tarian threaded his way through the tables, moving like a shark through water. His dark suit added to the severity of his appearance. Nothing softened the icy perfection of his beauty. But despite the fact he looked like he'd be comfortable heading a hostile boardroom takeover or stalking prey through a dark night, the humans in the restaurant were unable to look away.

*Nor am I,* she thought, butterflies fluttering in her

stomach. Tarian appeared oblivious of the stir he was causing. He had eyes only for her.

It'd been a long time since she'd been the center of such intense focus.

When he came close, she slipped to her feet.

"Hello, Tarian," she said, kissing the air above each cheek.

"Melissa." His hands traced lightly over her waist, but she felt the heat of his touch even through her dress.

"Am I late?" he asked, taking his seat. "Traffic was difficult."

"I got here early," she replied. "You're right on time."

A slight grin twisted his lips. "Couldn't stay away, hmm?"

There was no way the heat rising to her face could be a blush. She hadn't been flustered by a man in decades.

"What do you recommend?" he asked, picking up his menu.

Melissa shrugged. "Not really my forte but I hear the steak is good."

He glanced at her over the top of the menu. "Would you prefer to go somewhere else?"

"Oh no, I'm used to this. I'll just order an appetizer and pretend to pick at it all night."

Tarian arched a brow but made no further comment. "So you've been on Fated Match pairings before?" he asked as he perused his options.

She shook her head. "I only recently joined."

"Lucky me. I won't have years of competition to outdo."

She took a sip of water to hide her smile.

The waiter appeared at their side and took their orders. Melissa requested a salad for show and a glass of "fortified" wine. Though it appeared like a normal glass of red to an outside, human audience, in reality the liquid had the thicker consistency of blood.

"I must confess," Tarian said when the waiter left. "This is my first date through the agency. I just spent the past thirty minutes being debriefed on the dos and don'ts of the practice."

"Oh?" she asked. "What were some of the pitfalls to avoid?"

"It seemed that most of the rules revolved around minding my manners. Any sort of power or influence is banned on a first meeting. I'm to avoid controversial subjects like transformations, history in general, and interspecies politics."

"Do they suggest we discuss the weather and comment on safe topics such as the best places to see in the city or the adorable habits of mortals?"

"That would ensure I don't give any offense," he agreed.

"I'm not easily offended," she replied. "And Fated Match seems to have outlined the perfect recipe for a dull date."

"We wouldn't want that." His gaze bored into hers, though the half smile never left his lips.

"No," she purred. "We wouldn't."

The chatter around them fell away as she had eyes only for the man across from her. Again her body pulsed with anticipation. Had she been human, her heart would have been racing. Usually these dates were easy to guide. God knew she had more than enough practice at polite chitchat, but Tarian stole the words from her. She didn't want to speak of nothing. Instead a desire to know him filled her. Never before had she reacted so strongly to a man, and she needed to figure out just what it was about him that drew her. Was it a 90 percent rating thing, or was it something uniquely Tarian that drew her in?

Breaking her gaze, he reached into his briefcase. "I was also informed Fated Match follows the old tradition of intention gifts." He withdrew a small pink box and held it out to her.

Melissa accepted the package, which fit in the palm of her hand. She recognized the Fated Match logo stamped over the wrapping paper. In fact, she'd seen hundreds of identical boxes in Abbey's office. It was an old tradition, to be sure, but in times gone by supernatural creatures used to give little tokens to signal they were pursuing each other with a more permanent relationship in mind. Today Fated Match offered a discount gift service to members. A yearly fee would entitle the bearer to a gift box per date, all the items carefully selected by the Fated Match team to pair appropriate objects with the proper species requirements.

Her first dates through the agency had given her trinkets like small knickknacks or bottles of hand lotion. It was the intention that was important, more than the actual gift.

"This is very sweet of you," she said, pulling at the light-pink ribbon.

The sides of the box parted, and she wondered what lay within. Her money lay on the ever-popular scented candle.

But something shiny caught her eyes instead. Parting the folds of the box, she saw a beautiful silver bracelet nestled in the pink tissue paper.

"It's lovely," she breathed. This was no pre-selected Fated Match gift but one he had obviously thought of himself. Its beauty, however, didn't change one very large complication. "I love it. Really I do. But I can't keep it."

No expression crossed his face. "Why?" he asked as he

took a sip of his wine.

"Silver," she explained. "It burns my kind. I always wanted silver jewelry, but it's not possible for vampires."

"No?" He took another sip. "Touch it."

Melissa glanced up. "Silver feels like acid."

"Trust me."

Her eyes narrowed. What sort of game was this? It wouldn't help his cause to burn her on a first date. "I don't know you," she said. "Trust would be extremely foolish."

He held her gaze without comment. Melissa knew she should be handing the box back, but her fingers curled possessively around the paper. The urge to throw caution to the wind and trust him gripped her. As silly as it was, she wanted to take a chance on something new and different.

"I promise you won't get hurt," he assured her. "It was made for you."

She looked back to the delicate chain. It was a piece of art with its intricate Celtic design. She'd love to own a piece of jewelry like it.

Before she could think through the logic of her actions, Melissa lifted a hand toward the box. She hesitated a moment when her fingers hung over the gleaming surface. With one finger, she gingerly stroked the metal.

Nothing happened.

"What?" she said, shock swirling through her.

"It's spelled," he explained as he reached over and picked up the bracelet. "Allow me?"

Holding out her hand, Melissa watched as he clasped the silver around her wrist.

"I haven't owned silver in over a century," she said, still unable to believe her skin wasn't burning. "How did you do this?" If silver could be spelled this way, there was a fortune to be made in the jewelry market among her kind.

"Family secret," he replied. "Do you like it?"

"I love it," she said sincerely. "I think it might be the loveliest gift I've received in years."

"Excellent." He didn't release her wrist but trailed his fingers over her skin instead. "My matchmaker told me first impressions were important."

"You already made your first impression back at the agency," she replied, allowing her fingers to play over his skin as well.

"True. Must have been good for you to agree to meet me."

"We have a great match rating," she reminded him.

"Algorithm," he said. "I'm not sure how much stock I put in that."

"You think we aren't a good match?" She trailed her fingertips across his palm.

Heat flickered in his sapphire gaze. "On the contrary," he murmured. "Rating or not, I would have called you. The computer system is helpful, I suppose, but it doesn't replace seeing someone for the first time and knowing."

"Knowing what?"

A smile flashed over his face. "That she should be yours."

Desire shot through her. Oh yes, she knew exactly what he meant. Just as it had at Fated Match, proximity to this man filled her head with scandalous urges. Something about him resonated with her in a way no other man had accomplished in quite some time. If ever.

"Excuse me. Your meals," the waiter interrupted, appearing at their side.

Tarian released her, and she reluctantly drew her hand back.

A garden salad, which actually looked quite good, was set before her. Melissa knew from experience, though, that the leaves would be utterly tasteless if she put one in her mouth.

Instead she reached for the red glass the waiter had brought.

The first sip was ambrosia. Her eyes closed in pleasure as the warmed liquid washed over her tongue. Though she loved Abbey dearly, the mortal had never really understood her craving for blood. No human could. After the transformation, a single drop tasted like the best feast one had ever eaten as a human. To her, truly good blood almost reminded her of her first taste of chocolate.

"Good?" Tarian asked as he cut into his meat.

"Superb. I don't know what they infuse into the blood here, but maybe I should try hiring their cook." Melissa glanced at the glass in her hand before looking back to her date. "Does this bother you?"

He arched a brow as he chewed. "What do you mean?"

"Some people don't really approve of vampires eating in public." She'd dated a werewolf once who had insisted she only ever feed alone behind closed doors. He'd been scandalized by the idea that she'd love to bite him.

Tarian, however, looked unfazed. "I would never presume to tell a vampire when and where to commit an act they need to survive."

A sigh of relief escaped her. "Good to hear."

"I've never been uncomfortable around the world of death," he said, taking another bite. "You don't need to worry about me."

Except his words sparked a different kind of worry. "How comfortable are you, exactly?"

Another grin flashed her way. "Fishing for information, are we?"

"You have to admit, leaving your species section blank is going to raise some eyebrows."

"I don't want to be known just for my blood," he replied. "Don't you sometimes wish you could walk into a room and not be immediately recognized as Melissa Redgrave, vampire socialite?"

He had a point.

"Okay," she replied, taking another sip. "Just promise me your race is nothing dangerous that I should know about."

An emotion flashed across his eyes, but it was gone faster than she could track. "Promise," he said with a smile. "You're safe with me."

Melissa refrained from pointing out she was safe by herself. Her fangs and claws were sharp, and she had years of defense training under her belt. In fact, men's urges to see her as a delicate princess only served to piss her off on most occasions.

Which is why the warmth flooding her had to be pleasure from the blood and not from this stranger's words.

"All right then," she said. "If you are determined to be mysterious, then tell me what you think I should know about you."

He tilted his head to the side as he thought. "What you see is pretty much what you get," he said. "I'm a rather average man."

"Granted I've spent only a brief time with you, but

average is not the word I'd use."

His eyes flicked up to hers, and her grip tightened on the wine glass. Something about his gaze seemed to see into her. She didn't know if it was his magic or just simply him, but one thing was certain, nothing about this man was normal.

"Thank you for that," he said. "But I assure you my life is pretty staid. I moved east with my younger sister a few weeks ago. We were looking for a fresh start, and I hadn't been to New York since before the Empire State Building went up."

"It was quite the feat to watch," she said, remembering the wonder of its construction.

"I spent one lifetime as an architect," he told her. "It was possibly my favorite profession."

"But now you are in finance?"

He nodded. "A failing economy is bad for supernaturals as well as humans. I have the skills to be useful, so why not work in the sector for now? Perhaps I'll go back to architecture in a few decades."

Melissa thought of her long life. Though she'd had the odd job here and there, being Lucian's heir had provided a very different way of living. She'd been more of a patron than a worker for most of her life. Even now she was following that pre-determined role.

"So you see," Tarian said, breaking her from her thoughts. "There is not much to tell about me."

It was on the tip of her tongue to ask about his age, but she bit back the impolite question. Most supernaturals didn't like to discuss such matters, and either way it was a moot point. For Tarian, she'd been willing to overlook her age gap rule.

"Where were you before the city?"

He focused his attention on his food. "We moved around quite a bit. There isn't much of this country I haven't seen."

"And before that?"

Tarian glanced up at her, but his expressive gaze was shuttered. "Let's just say I've spent more than a few lifetimes on this continent and leave it at that. Unless, of course, you wish to tell me intimate details of your past in exchange for stories from mine."

She smiled slightly. "I was being rude. My apologies."

He shook his head. "While I appreciate the interest, there are parts of my life I prefer not discussing. I'm sure it is the same with you."

The accident flashed across her mind as she inclined her head. "On to more mannered subjects then," she said. "I hope you enjoy your time in New York."

"It's definitely growing on me," he replied, eying her.

The fresh blood circulating in her body made it easier to blush. That was the only reason her cheeks were heating.

"What about you?" Tarian asked. "What do I need to know about the famous Melissa Redgrave?"

She made a face. "That I don't like the attention, for one."

"Not a fan of the spotlight?"

Melissa took a sip from her glass. "I suppose I don't really know any alternative. My human life ended abruptly, and my immortal one had only ever been lived as Lucian's sole heir."

"It must be grating that people make assumptions about you before even meeting."

"Exactly," she agreed. "There are times when I want to shout that I'm not just a mirror image of my father. I have my own ideas."

Tarian chewed slowly as he nodded. "It is important not to make snap decisions. People are more complex than a bloodline."

It was rare to hear someone understand her thinking and not simply smile and agree with anything she said just because she had Lucian on speed dial.

"You should be warned," she said, "sticking with me will shine the spotlight on you as well."

Tarian's gaze slid away from her, and for a moment she feared she'd scared him away. Not everyone wanted their face plastered on the front of magazines. If he was a man who valued his privacy, dating her could be a problem.

But when he looked back at her, there was a smile on his face. "I'm not easily dissuaded from things I want," he told her. "And a few articles are a small price to pay to see you again."

Pleasure filled her. "Glad to hear it," she said, tapping her wine glass against his.

"I take it you enjoy your work with the Redgrave foundation?"

"I do," she replied. "It's something I seem to be good at, but every now and then…" Her voice trailed off.

He arched an inquiring brow, popping a carrot into his mouth.

Melissa leaned forward to rest her arms on the table. "I want to do more than plan parties and hold events. My father is always caught up in making important policy changes that help govern our world, and I have no part of that branch of the Redgrave responsibilities."

"What would you change?"

She sighed, shaking her head. "I don't know. I plan other people's charities but I have no cause of my own."

"Nothing to fight for."

"Exactly." Melissa leaned back. "But I suppose I'm too young to be of any real use to my father. I haven't had time to learn about all the inner workings of our world."

"I disagree," Tarian replied. "Your youth gives you fresh eyes. Allows you to look at problems from a different perspective. Is there nothing facing your father you could assist with?"

Melissa scoffed. "He's dealing with the necromancers. Not an area I'd be inclined to offer 'fresh eyes' on."

Tarian paused in mid chew. "No," he replied, his voice subdued. "I suppose not."

Melissa studied her companion as she tipped the last swallow of blood to her lips. He scraped up the last of his potatoes before setting his cutlery on the empty place.

"Was it good?" she asked with a smile.

"Wonderful," he replied. "I'll have to remember this place."

"There are several restaurants that cater to our kind, but Celeste's reigns supreme."

"Dessert?" he asked.

She shook her head. While they did have a delightful blood sorbet, she couldn't eat another drop. "I'm completely satisfied."

When a knowing smile tugged at his lips, she mentally amended the statement. Her hunger for blood was completely satisfied. Her hunger for him, however, was only growing.

"Then let me grab the check," he offered, flagging down

the waiter.

Melissa leaned back in her seat. Usually she offered to split the bill, but it tended to annoy the more old-fashioned immortals. Given how well the night was going, she decided to let this time slide.

"Thank you for dinner," she said as he signed the bill and handed it back to the waiter.

"It was my pleasure," he replied, offering a hand to help her stand.

Though unnecessary, Melissa would take any chance she could get to touch him.

She slipped her fingers into his and rose from the chair. This close, she had to tilt her head up to see him, despite her heels.

"We'll have to do it again sometime," she breathed.

Tarian raised her hand to his lips and pressed a light kiss to her knuckles. "Agreed."

With him keeping hold of her hand, they navigated their way through the restaurant. Melissa grinned at the envious glances being thrown her way. Logic told her he'd be going on other Fated Match dates, but tonight he felt like he was hers alone.

Together they stepped into the night, and she inhaled the cool air out of habit rather than necessity.

"Full moon," she said, looking at the sky. "There'll be weres running around Central Park tonight."

"No doubt," he agreed from by her side.

Leaving the bright sky, she transferred her gaze to her date.

"So," she said, unsure of what to say.

A grin flashed across his lips. "So." He turned to face

her, still keeping a hold of her hand.

Nerves gripped her as she looked up at him. It was ridiculous at her age to be acting like a schoolgirl out with her first crush. She'd perfected the art of suave seduction, but Tarian made her forget all her tricks.

He stepped forward, crowding her against the brick wall.

"I was told 48 percent of first dates don't end in a good night kiss. I think that's an appalling statistic."

"Absolutely terrible," she agreed. "We should do our best to offset the data."

She caught a brief view of his grin before his mouth claimed hers.

Melissa's eyes closed as she twined her arms around his shoulders. His lips trailed over hers with tantalizing gentleness. She knew he was teasing her, and though she enjoyed the play, she pushed up on her tiptoes to demand more.

The light teasing left his touch as he took possession of her mouth. Her lips parted for him and welcomed his questing tongue.

Tarian's hands slid over her hips to cup her waist. He pulled her against his hard body and she moaned against his mouth. Fire flared through her as she kissed him. In the back of her mind, she pictured them making out like teenagers on a very exposed street corner but didn't care. All she could think about was the pressure of his mouth, the heat from his hands.

Her fangs ached in her gums. What would it be like to drive them into his neck as he drove into her body? The thought melted her into a puddle of need. Whatever it was about this addicting man, she had no resistance to him.

"More," she purred against his mouth, her hands trailing

down his chest. Hooking her fingers around his belt loops, she pulled him close, rubbing against his straining erection.

"My apartment is close," she offered. She nipped his lower lip lightly before leaning back to see his face.

"How close?" he growled.

"Very." Rising back to her tiptoes, she pressed a gossamer kiss to his lips.

His hands tightened on her waist. "We shouldn't."

"I think we really, really should." Melissa leaned forward for another taste when her arms were magically empty. "Seriously?" she demanded, glaring at the man now standing four feet from her.

"I was thoroughly warned about first date etiquette," he replied.

She was going to kill Abbey.

"What do they know?" she argued, closing the distance between them.

He cupped her face, staring down at her with a tenderness she couldn't remember seeing in another man's eyes. "I have work to do tonight, sweetheart, not to mention I don't want to do anything to derail this."

"What?"

"Us." He kissed her softly.

"Trust me, great sex had never doomed any of my relationships."

He laughed, releasing her. "Anticipation, my dear. I'm worth the wait."

He had better be. No one turned her down. Maybe she was losing her touch.

"I'll call you tomorrow," he said.

She sighed in defeat. "Fine. Tomorrow. But don't make

me wait too long."

Tarian chuckled and treated her to a last toe-curling kiss. "Let me hail you a cab."

She shook her head. "I've got a town car waiting."

"Then until tomorrow, Ms. Redgrave." He swept her a bow that again made her question his age. He might be more lively than the ancients she knew but he sure had some old-fashioned ideas.

"Good night." With a last, lingering glance, she set off down the street to her car. She couldn't help looking back over her shoulder and grinned when she saw he was watching her.

Fishing her cell out of her purse, she quickly texted Abbey.

*You found a winner,* she typed. *Fill you in when I'm home.*

Smiley faces and exclamation marks filled her screen as her friend replied. Putting her phone away, she rounded the corner and spotted her car.

Melissa knew she was grinning like a lunatic but couldn't do a thing to stop herself. Maybe, after all these decades, her luck was finally starting to change.

# Chapter Four

It was impossible to concentrate on work.

Melissa shook her head before focusing on the computer once more. She had too much to do, and spending every free moment thinking about Tarian wasn't helping.

He'd called earlier so they could make dinner plans for tomorrow night. It had seemed like a good idea at the time, since she hadn't wanted to appear too eager, and she had a pile of work to get through today. Hours later, however, she wished she'd found a way to play hooky. A date a day might be a little extreme but she wasn't too proud to admit she wanted to see him as much as she could.

*A day apart will do you good.* She'd already ruined one document by doodling his name in the corner of it. Melissa needed to get a grip on herself before she saw him again. Hell, in her current state of eagerness she might scare him off, and that was the last thing she wanted to do.

"Your midnight appointment, Ms. Redgrave."

She didn't even bother glancing up from her computer. Though her secretary was rarely wrong, she'd made an error this time. Melissa had gone through the schedule backward and forward to see if she could justify taking an early night to see Tarian.

"I don't have a midnight today, Mary," she called. "But I will take the files on the Miller gala when you have a moment."

"She means she'll take them after her lunch break," a deep voice cut in.

Abandoning her charity files, she looked up to see Tarian standing in her doorway.

"What are you doing here?" she asked, pushing from her chair. "We don't have plans until tomorrow."

"I realize you're busy, but I couldn't wait." His hands slid over her hips as she stepped up to kiss him hello.

"This is an excellent surprise," she murmured as her lips touched his. Conscious of her glass door and the eager eyes of her secretary, Melissa forced herself to keep the kiss chaste despite the fire roiling through her with just one touch.

Stepping back, she smoothed her hands over the dark material of his lapel. She hadn't thought to see him tonight, but now that he was here, standing before her, she had to fight to keep a silly, happy grin off her face.

"Want to hear my master plan?" Tarian asked.

"Enlighten me."

He held up a brown paper bag. "Even people as dedicated as you need a lunch break. I thought I'd tempt you with some food and excellent company."

"And I've pushed back your next appointment," Mary

threw in.

Melissa arched a brow at the designer sandwich bag sitting on her secretary's desk. "Did you bribe Mary?"

"Shamelessly," he agreed. "She was a wealth of information, not only about your schedule, but also on your favorite take out places." He leaned close enough to whisper in her ear as he added, "She's also promised not to turn around or let anyone near your office."

"Has she?" Melissa purred. "I knew she was an invaluable hire."

"Come on," Tarian said as he caught her hand. He led her over to the small couch she couldn't remember ever using. Lounging back on the beige upholstery, Tarian offered a delicious contrast in his tailored black suit. She was a sucker for an impeccable dresser, and Tarian was definitely a man who knew how to wear his clothes.

"What did you bring?" she asked as she sank down beside him.

"A sandwich for me and some blood for you." He unpacked the bag onto the coffee table before them.

Melissa reached for the travel cup of blood and saw her favorite restaurant's name blazed across the plastic.

"I must confess," Tarian said as he unwrapped his sandwich, "I didn't know there was a difference when it came to blood."

"Every person has their own unique taste but you're right, when it comes to bagged blood it's all pretty much the same."

"So why did Mary have me tracking down this particular brand?"

"In the past decade or so chefs have been experimenting

with making feeding a little less monotonous for vampires."

"It'd be a huge market," he agreed.

She took a sip of the gently warmed blood and closed her eyes in pure delight. "They mix spices and flavors into the blood to give it a bit of oomph, and this just happens to be my favorite."

Melissa opened her eyes to see her date staring at her with a lopsided smile. "I have to say," he murmured, "that sight might just have been worth racing around the city."

Heat warmed her cheeks as she looked down. "Well, I appreciate the effort."

He shrugged as he ate. "This is a welcome break for me, too."

"Plus you are scoring major brownie points."

"A wise man plans ahead," he teased.

"Are you planning to screw this up any time soon?"

His smile slipped a notch even as he shook his head. "Screwing things up with you is not an option I want to contemplate."

She kicked off her Manolo Blahniks and tugged her legs up under her. The skirt of her royal blue business dress rode up, but she didn't bother correcting the slip. Instead she enjoyed the way Tarian's eyes locked on the flash of skin.

"You seem to be off to an excellent start," she said, leaning closer.

"Sweetheart, you make a man want to put in some extra effort."

She took a sip of her blood and refrained from commenting on all the men in her past that would dispute Tarian's words.

"Be that as it may, no one has ever crashed my office

before."

"The idea of staring at my phone for hours on end when I could be staring at you was far too tempting an opportunity to pass up."

"Fishing for a text, were we?"

He inclined his head. "I don't even like this new cell phone trend and there I was, walking around with the damned thing in my pocket at all times."

Melissa didn't need to glance at her desk to know her own phone sat next to her keyboard, positioned so she would see it the second a text came in.

"The art of romance is no match for the generation of iPhones and cat videos," she said.

His fingers twined through hers. "Exactly. What happened to the good old days of penned love letters and clandestine meetings?"

"When a simple touch could have your heart racing," she purred, drawing the tips of her fingers along his palm.

"And a kiss could change everything." He leaned forward and Melissa allowed him to push her backward into the couch.

"Are you sure you bribed Mary well enough to give us our privacy?" she asked, angling her head back toward the glass doors of her office.

"I added the world's most decadent brownie to her order."

"Machiavelli would be proud."

His lips crashed down onto hers. Smiling against his mouth, Melissa wrapped her arms around his muscled shoulders and gave herself up to the pleasure of his touch. His tongue teased along the seam of her lips, demanding entry even as his hand slid over the curve of her hip. Opening her mouth, she greeted Tarian's questing tongue with her own eager caresses.

Melissa shifted under him to better fit his body against hers. Even as she moved, she knew she should be thinking about the full office outside her doors. There was work to be done. Meetings to prep for and files to be read. She'd put Tarian off until tomorrow for a reason.

But right now with his hands on her body she couldn't remember why she hadn't leapt at any chance to see him again.

Her fingers raked down his back, clawing at cloth when she wanted to feel skin. One of his hands slid up her hose-covered thigh. He was undeterred by her skirt's hem and merely pushed under it instead.

Not once, in all the years she'd worked, had any man so much as kissed her in this office, let alone engaged in a good old-fashioned make out session. The rational section of her mind demanded she put a stop to this nonsense.

But a far more powerful part of her reveled in Tarian's attentions. He'd been all she could think about since they'd parted ways yesterday. The man had filled her daylight dreams and consumed her waking thoughts. She'd been counting down the hours till she'd be able to see him.

His hands gripped her thighs, pushing them apart as he shifted more intimately against her. The couch was by no means wide, but Melissa didn't mind the close contact. When his mouth trailed a burning path down her throat she arched under him, tilting her head back to give him better access.

Her fangs ached to explode from her gums, but she held back. Miss Manners would certainly frown at heavy petting for lunch, and Melissa didn't even want to imagine what the woman would have to say about biting on a second date.

The knowledge that she had no business lusting after Tarian's blood didn't quell the desire. It usually took months to get to the point where she'd be comfortable feeding from a lover. Longer sometimes to convince her partners to accept such an intimate act.

Yet here she was with a man she barely knew, breaking all her rules.

"What is it about you?" she breathed as he cupped her breasts through her dress.

Why did he make her crave things she had no business dreaming about? It was too soon to need him this badly, to lust for his body and his blood in equal measure.

That secret, troublemaking corner of her mind whispered that attraction was always intense between mates. Her father had been unable to think of anything but Abbey once the couple had met.

Melissa shook her head to clear the impossible thought. Whatever Tarian and she were to each other, it was far too early to even contemplate the M word.

*Lover*, however, was a word she'd be more than happy to consider.

"You really should have come home with me last night," she whispered in his ear.

"A mistake I'll regret for a long time to come," he replied. "I was trying to be a gentleman."

"Does that mean I have to be a lady?" She reached down to stroke her fingers along the erection straining from his trousers.

His swift inhalation brought a smile to her lips.

"You can be whatever the hell you want to be."

*What if I want to be yours?*

She cleared her throat and pushed back the rogue thought. "Right now," she said, pressing a hand to his chest, "I want to be professional."

He allowed her to push him off of her, though he arched a brow at her words. "Want?"

Her lips twitched. "Need," she amended.

Tarian ran a hand through his tousled hair. "Understood. I want it noted I hadn't intended to seduce you in your rather exposed office."

"No?"

His boyish smile made an appearance as he righted his jacket. "Hoped is not the same as planned."

Melissa wiggled her dress back into place and patted her hair. "Do I look like we've been doing naughty things?"

"You look perfect," he replied, reaching out to tuck a curl back into place.

The mixture of lust and tenderness in his eyes would have made her heart race if it still had the ability.

"We could just hang out at my place tomorrow," she suggested. "I can dazzle you with my cooking skills."

"You cook?"

She shrugged. "I microwave. And when I have people over who consume food, I am a takeout ordering queen."

His laughter filled the room, and an inordinate amount of pride filled her that she'd caused such a wonderful sound to emerge.

"How about we make it a quick dinner?" he compromised. "Then back to your place."

"Not going to fight me this time?"

"Never again," he said. "Gentlemanly behavior be damned."

"Excellent news." She leaned over to press her lips to his.

It was a light touch. One meant to promise rather than enflame, but even so, Melissa didn't want to pull back.

*Tomorrow,* she told herself. Once she had him in her apartment she could explore his body at her leisure.

"I should go," he said against her mouth. "We're running out of time."

"I know." She sat back with a sigh as he scooped his half-eaten sandwich back into its brown bag. "Looks like the concept of lunch got a little lost on us."

He tossed her a grin. "I'm not complaining."

"Me, either," she said as they stood.

"Till tomorrow then."

"Tomorrow," she agreed. "I can't wait."

He took her hand and pressed his lips to her knuckles. "Neither can I." With a last heated look, he strode from her office.

Melissa had barely managed to make her way back to her desk when Mary swept in with files for her perusal.

"Good lunch?" her assistant asked.

"The best," she sighed.

"He's got damn fine taste in chocolate," Mary said. "An excellent quality in a man."

"The list of his excellent qualities is rapidly growing. I'm half waiting for the other shoe to drop."

Mary shrugged. "Unless it's one hell of a shoe, I doubt it'll make much difference."

"You are, as usual, correct." Accepting the files she shooed Mary from the office.

When it came to Tarian, she had the suspicion she'd be willing to forgive a hell of a lot. A smile curved her lips as she attempted to focus on her work once more. Tomorrow she'd just have to try and uncover more of his secrets. After she got the man in bed, of course.

Grinning, she glanced at the clock on her wall and wished that time would move just a little bit faster.

• • •

Tarian sighed as the elevator doors closed behind him.

"Damn," he whispered into the empty space.

He'd come there tonight half hoping their first date had been a fluke. After all, no necromancer could really be that interested in a vampire so quickly. Even if that vampire was as close to perfection as he'd found in hundreds of years.

Except seeing Melissa again only underscored what he'd felt the night before. He liked being around her, and not just because he'd love to spread her out across his bed. No, it was far more insidious than that. He liked her unique mix of confidence and uncertainty. The blushes that stained her cheeks even when she tried to appear unaffected. The way she lit up when she spoke about the charities she worked with.

His instinctive reaction to her may have driven him to see her at Celeste's, but tonight he'd hunted her down because he couldn't stand not to.

"Grandfather will have a heyday with this," he murmured.

He'd woken this morning to find a list of reasons to fight against the vampires taped to his bathroom mirror. Eilin was far more passionate about the cause than he'd given her credit for. Then again, he well remembered what it was like to be young and blinded by hatred. Maybe he should take her and run. Leave New York behind and hide his sister from their grandfather's bloody crusade.

Tarian closed his eyes. That would mean moving yet again. Hopping from city to city trying to stay a step ahead of his family. After running for so many years he was just...

Tired.

New York was their fresh start and he wanted to make the most of it. See what life could be like with a permanent address. Living here might be an impossible dream for a necromancer, but he'd had enough of his bloodline limiting his choices.

The elevator doors opened, and he strode out into the lobby. He could afford to give the situation another week or two. If Eilin showed any more signs of wanting to throw her lot in with their kin, then he'd whisk her away. Until then, there was no use upending their lives again when they'd just gotten settled.

*Two weeks,* he thought. More than enough time to see where this connection with Melissa was leading. Hell, maybe they'd both get lucky and it would amount to nothing more than a few nights of great sex and an amicable parting of ways.

He stepped out into the crisp night air and did his best to ignore the fact that he rather doubted it.

• • •

"But how did you know?"

Abbey's chuckle rose from the phone's speakers.

"I very much doubt you want me to go into intimate

detail about my own mating," Abbey said. "After all, it's your father we're talking about."

"Yes, yes, I appreciate your discretion." Getting a straight answer out of her friend was like pulling teeth. Melissa had spent her hours since waking trying on dress after dress, hunting for the perfect outfit for her date tonight. She would have loved to have Abbey there, not only as a second set of eyes, but also so she could pick the other woman's brain when it came to discovering mates. Abbey, however, was tied up at work, so a quick phone call was all she could spare.

Melissa tapped the speakerphone icon on her cell before tossing it onto the bed. "I was speaking in more general terms. How did you know Lucian was the one for you?"

Standing in front of her full-length mirror, she eyed the A-line lacy white dress with a critical eye. Though it fit her slender frame, it was a tad too innocent for the vibe she was hoping to project tonight.

"I didn't," Abbey's voice rose from the bed. "Not really. It took me a long time to come to terms with what Lucian and I were to each other. And it took your father even longer than that."

She tugged the dress over her head before rummaging through her closet. "How did you feel when you first met him? When you first went out with him?"

Grabbing a sexy black cocktail dress, she shimmied into it.

"I felt…" Abbey's voice trailed off into a small, helpless laugh.

Melissa paused. That sound, the light, confused yet happy laugh exactly fit the coil of emotions she was trying to name.

"I felt off balance," Abbey said. "He consumed my thoughts. My heart raced just being in the same room with him."

"Did you feel more attracted to him than anyone else in a long time?"

Another laugh escaped her friend. "I've never needed anyone the way I do Lucian."

Melissa smoothed a hand over the sinful black dress as she examined her reflection. It hugged her body in all the right ways while being demure enough to justify wearing to dinner. Butterflies filled her stomach at the thought of seeing Tarian in less than an hour.

"Does this phone call have anything to do with your date tonight?" Abbey asked.

"You know me. I like to have all the facts before entering into any new enterprise."

"Finding your mate has very little to do with logic or facts."

The words were nothing new. Her father had said much the same thing when he'd fallen for a human. Still, she couldn't help wishing there was some magical way to know in advance whether Tarian would work out.

"Thanks for the chat, Abbey, but I've got to get across town."

"Call me once your date's over. I want to hear all the juicy details."

"Promise," she said. "Talk to you later." She disconnected the call before throwing the phone into her black clutch. With one last look in the mirror to ensure everything was in place, she swept from her bedroom.

As she walked down the hall to the main door she did a

mental review of her apartment. The living room was picked up, and her bed had new sheets. The kitchen was clean, not that dishes in the sink were ever much of a problem with her. The place was ready to entertain some company and so was she.

Melissa checked her watch as she left the apartment. Less than half an hour before she was supposed to meet Tarian. Her driver had his work cut out for him tonight.

She took the elevator down to the parking level and stepped out to see her town car already waiting for her.

The driver stepped from the car as she approached and opened the back door for her.

"Thanks for coming, Luke," she said as she drew closer.

Luke didn't respond.

A frown crossed her face as her steps slowed.

"Luke?"

Still no response.

Her instincts flared to life. Her driver didn't have a quiet bone in his body. Nothing stopped his incessant flow of chatter.

Something wasn't right.

But before she could run, bodies burst from the cars around her. Shadows surrounded her, grabbing her arms and holding her down.

"Use your powers," someone said.

"It isn't bloody working," another replied.

Fangs sprang to life in her mouth and claws shot from her fingertips as she fought her captors. She heard a cry of pain and grinned in feral satisfaction for having wounded one until a sharp prick hit her arm. The sight of a depressed syringe filled her vision even as the world started to spin around her.

Her struggles slowed and grew sluggish. Melissa tried to keep her eyes open but against the drug, there was nothing she could do.

The pavement rose up to meet her as she fell into utter blackness.

# Chapter Five

"Call on line two, Mr. Drake."

Tarian waved to the secretary before reaching for his phone. "Drake speaking," he greeted the caller, turning back to the spreadsheets littering the desk in front of him. "How can I help you?"

"Mr. Drake, this is Abbey from Fated Match."

He set the pen down and leaned back in his chair. "Hello, Abbey."

"I need to ask you a few questions about your date with Ms. Redgrave."

There was a strain to the matchmaker's voice that seemed at odds with her usual cheery disposition. "What's wrong?"

"You saw her last night, correct?"

He frowned. "Actually, I didn't. We had plans to meet, but she never showed up. I tried to call but couldn't get through. I assumed some emergency had come up. She didn't strike me as the type to just leave me hanging."

"No, she's not. Mr. Drake, Melissa never came home last night. Her driver is also missing. I believe you were one of the last people to see her. Did she mention anything about going somewhere?"

Ice slithered down his spine. "As far as I knew the only place she was planning on going was to the restaurant with me."

Abbey sighed into the phone. "Then I apologize for what's coming your way. Melissa's father will not take her disappearance lightly, and as soon as night falls I guarantee he'll be paying you a visit."

"Redgrave," he said. The most powerful vampire in the city. If anyone would be able to sniff out his necromancer blood, it'd be Lucian.

"I swear we don't normally have such drama at Fated Match but safety is our primary concern."

"Of course. Please let me know if there is anything I can do to help."

"Thank you. If Melissa contacts you, please let me know."

The phone went dead as Abbey hung up.

For a moment he sat frozen in his chair. Melissa missing. Right before she was supposed to have met him. It looked bad from every angle. Add in his heritage and it was a disaster.

*Who knew where we'd be?* he thought. *The agency didn't divulge that information. Melissa could have mentioned it to a friend. And I—*

"Goddamn it." Grabbing the phone, he dialed a number by heart.

"Hello?" Eilin answered.

"What did you do?"

Silence reigned.

Fury sizzled through him, banishing the cold shock. "Tell me this wasn't you, Eilin."

"Grandfather said it was our best chance."

Tarian bit back the curse on the tip of his tongue. "You will start a war."

"We just want to ransom her to her father. No fuss, no muss."

"If you believe that, then you are more of a child than I thought," he replied, jumping to his feet. Grabbing his jacket from the back of his chair and his briefcase from the floor, he strode out of the office like a storm.

"Where did they take her?"

"I'm not supposed to tell you."

"Dammit, Eilin. Let me undo this mess before someone ends up dead. Where is Melissa?"

He could imagine his sister chewing on her lip in indecision. "I'm the last family you've got," he hissed into the phone. "And if she dies, I will never forgive you for this."

"She's just a leech." But the conviction in Eilin's voice was wavering.

"You knew about my date, little sister. Not only have you put a genuinely decent woman in harm's way, you made me an accomplice to this abduction. No one will believe I wasn't a part of it. You might be ready to destroy a vampire's life but are you ready to destroy mine?"

Another heartbeat of silence.

"Eilin."

"The ranch," she whispered.

Tarian punched the elevator call button. "You flew her

across state lines?"

"Everyone thought it would be best to keep her far away from her father."

"Listen to me, Eilin. I will fix this, but you don't leave the apartment until I'm back. You hear me? Necromancers will be the first people they blame for this. And rightly damn so."

"Promise." Her voice was small, lacking the certainty it had first held.

He disconnected without saying goodbye.

As he rode down the elevator he told himself he'd be this enraged if any other vampire had been kidnapped, but he knew the truth. The idea of Melissa in danger twisted something inside of him. That her date with him had given her captors their opportunity slayed him.

"I'll find her," he vowed.

And somehow stop the vampire community from eradicating his race in the process.

• • •

Voices tuned in and out. A blur of shapes moved around her, but she couldn't force her eyes open.

"Dose her again," someone said. "We've got a ways to go."

"We don't want to damage her," someone argued.

"You'd rather fight a vampire on a plane?" the first voice snapped. "We'll all crash."

"Why can't we control her?" a female voice mused.

"A problem for a later date."

Pain flared in her arm again, and blackness claimed her once more.

When she opened her eyes again, she was no longer on a moving plane but instead in a soft bed.

Melissa pushed herself up, groaning as her brain pounded in protest.

"What the hell?" she hissed, clutching her head.

"That would be the deadman's thistle," a voice said. "I hear it affects vampires much like chloroform does humans."

Despite the pain in her head, she launched herself off the bed. Claws burst from her fingernails, and fangs exploded in her mouth. "Who are you?"

An older man sat completely at ease on an armchair across the room. He watched her with calm brown eyes. Though tiny wrinkles ringed his mouth and white had started to pepper his black hair, she would not mistake this man for being anything other than a threat. Power radiated from him, the kind of magic only very old beings could command.

Shifting around the bed, she sidestepped until the wall was at her back.

"I thought you'd like the room," the man said. "Complete blackout curtains for the window of course."

She glanced around the spacious chamber to ensure they were alone. If the Mad Hatter had ever yearned to be an interior decorator, he might have created a room rather like this one.

A canopied bed dominated the space, complete with the lace and frills every little girl would envy. Though the theme of the room seemed to be a Victorian tea party, everything clashed, from the yellow wallpaper to the shaggy pink carpet.

Two things were apparent about the room. First, it was wired for security. She saw the camera above the door and the bars on the windows. Second, nothing would make a decent weapon. Old wooden furniture and lacy bed sheets were the extent of her arsenal.

"What am I doing here?" she demanded.

The man wrapped his hands around the black cane he carried and pushed to his feet. "You are a guest."

"Yours?"

He sketched her an elegant bow. "Dominic Salverg, at your service."

"You kidnapped me."

"Yes," he agreed. "Unfortunate business to be sure, but I needed to get your father's attention. We need to start a new relationship between your people and mine."

She swallowed. "Who are your people?"

A brief grin flashed across his face, "Why, the necromancers, of course."

Melissa was no stranger to danger. Growing up as the daughter of a Redgrave ensured her world was never boring, but facing a necromancer sent fear shooting through her entire body.

"Now, about that," he said, taking a step toward her. "It seems that during your, shall we say, recruitment, you showed a surprising resistance to our powers."

She blinked. That wasn't possible.

"How did you do it, child?"

"Even if I knew, do you think I'd tell you?" she snapped.

He shrugged. "I was being polite, but we will get to the bottom of this." Moving to the door, he rapped his knuckles on the shining wood.

The door opened to a group of people, none of whom looked remotely friendly. Melissa shifted to keep them in her line of sight. There were too many to fight. She was woefully outnumbered.

"Susanne here has quite the gift when it comes to magic and is sympathetic to our cause," Dominic said, gesturing to a small, dark-haired witch. "As vampires cannot develop a natural immunity, our leading theory is that you've been enspelled."

"Not that I know of." But then again, she had no explanation for this resistance either. Not that she'd be willing to give it up.

Susanne stepped forward. She might be small, but her green eyes were hard. Looked like vampires were not wildly popular in this house.

The witch stretched out her hand and Melissa felt a flood of magic wash over her. It wasn't an uncomfortable feeling, but alien and unwelcome, like fingernails scraping against her skin.

"There," the woman said, wiggling her fingers.

Metal slid against her wrist and Melissa looked down to see her silver bracelet unclasp by itself. She made a lunge to catch it, but the trinket flew across the room into the witch's hand.

"Hmm," Susanne said, studying the accessory. "This was the problem."

Dominic limped over to touch the bracelet. "She wore a rield?"

"A what?" Melissa demanded.

"Rield," he replied, turning his attention to her. "They are very rare and very hard to craft. Only the most powerful necromancers can create them."

For a moment she was at a loss for words. She'd never heard of necromancers having the ability to create a shield from their powers because, really, why would they ever bother? Their power lay in their ability to manipulate the dead. Giving a vampire a shield would strip a necromancer of their greatest weapon.

"Who gave you this bracelet, Melissa?"

Tarian's face flashed across her mind. Had he known? Fear clutched her heart. He'd refused to tell her his race, after all. But as soon as the panic gripped her, it faded. The idea of him being a necromancer was ridiculous. He never would have willingly pursued a vampire, let alone kissed her the way he had. And if he'd been her enemy, he'd never have given her such a powerful weapon against him. Especially not at a first meeting.

But how had he come across it in the first place?

"Vampire, who gave you the rield?" The friendly Southern charm had dropped from Dominic's voice.

"My father," she lied. "Who else would be able to find something like that?"

"Damn Redgrave," Dominic muttered, pocketing the bracelet. "Well, at least that's one problem solved."

He flicked his fingers at her, and ice swept through her body. Melissa tried to open her mouth, but she couldn't move. She couldn't even blink. Dominic's magic sank into her like a second skin.

"Come here," he said.

Melissa wanted to tell him to go to hell but instead, her feet moved forward. No matter how she screamed in her mind, her body refused to obey. It glided toward the necromancer with natural grace. Someone watching her would never know she wasn't in control of her own actions.

"Perfect," Dominic said. "Come down for dinner with us, Melissa. We have quite a bit to talk about."

Her lips stretched into a polite smile when all she wanted to do was rip him to shreds.

Instead, she turned and walked out of the door. She swept down the hall completely surrounded by her people's worse nightmare.

Though she'd been sure she was walking to her doom, Dominic really had just ordered her to dinner. A massive table had been set with easily twenty places. Her seat was just to the right of Dominic. After ensuring she was seated, the necromancer's magic had faded away, leaving her able to move.

Not that she had many options. Running to the door would have been a waste of effort in a room full of people who could stop her with a thought. All she could do was sit in silence as the group ate.

A glass of blood was placed before her, but she made no move to touch it. Though she needed to replenish her strength, she didn't trust these people not to drug her again.

A wide window cut into the wall opposite her, treating her to a night view of desert wasteland beyond the house. Where was she? Arizona? Texas? Certainly not New York, that was for sure. Just another nail in her coffin. Lucian wouldn't even know where to look for her.

Halfway through their first course, Dominic finally turned his attention back to her. "Is the blood not to your liking?"

She glanced at her chillingly solicitous host. "Not hungry," she lied.

"Nonsense. Drink."

Her hand reached out of its own accord and brought the glass to her lips. She swallowed twice before her hand set the blood back down.

"See, this won't be so bad," Dominic said. "I doubt you'll be here more than a few days, and now that the rield problem is taken care of, you will have full reign of the house. Though I caution you, this home is always full. Someone will be close to you at all times if you choose to make…poor decisions."

"What do you want with my father?" she asked.

"To broker an exchange, so to speak." Dominic cut a precise piece of meat and popped it in his mouth. "Your father is the vampire elder of New York."

"Yes." It was common knowledge. Each faction of supernatural had an ancient representative speaking on behalf of their people. Lucian was, for all intents and purposes, the king of the undead in New York.

"He has the power to give us what we want."

"Which is?"

"Why, a home." He took a sip of his wine.

Melissa waited, but Dominic seemed to be finished with his explanation. "What do you mean, home?" she said. "What's this then?"

"Not a house, child," he said. Though his smile remained in place, his eyes were blank. She'd seen gazes like that before and never in well-adjusted, peaceful individuals. "For centuries necromancers have been unwelcome in the supernatural community merely because of the threat we pose to the leading race. To avoid further conflict, we took our banishment in silence and did our best to stay away. We stick to rural areas. We scatter to avoid detection. Well, no longer. We want New York."

"The…the city?"

"Precisely. You for the city. Finally we'll have a place where we can live in peace. Vampires can go anywhere. You'll be fine."

"But…do you have any idea how many vampires live and work in the city?"

"Do you have any idea how many necromancers are currently living on the fringes of society?" he replied.

"My father isn't going to be able clear out an entire city of vampires. Not to mention the rest of the elder council won't help support such a takeover. And certainly not over one vampire hostage."

"For your sake, Melissa, I hope you are wrong."

She looked away from the dead eyes staring at her. Dominic wasn't the sort of man to be dissuaded from his plan by anything she said.

And her father wasn't the sort to give in to threats. She had no doubt Lucian loved her utterly and completely, but he wouldn't uproot hundreds of lives for her.

She was well and truly screwed.

*I have to escape,* she reasoned. That was the only way out of this. Their plan required a Redgrave hostage. If she could just get away, they would have nothing to bargain with.

But how?

She looked down the table at the necromancers eating. A little girl sat near the end with her mother and a drop of sympathy touched her heart. No doubt necromancer children led hard lives, but they grew up into the nightmares of her people. They didn't deserve New York. Hell, they should be grateful the rest of the supernatural world didn't hunt them down and eradicate their frightening powers.

Movement caught the corner of her eye, and she turned to see a man hurrying toward Dominic.

Dominic gestured him closer and listened while the man whispered in his ear.

"What do you mean he's here?" Dominic demanded.

She arched a brow, wishing her sensitive hearing could pick up the other man's words.

"I suppose there's no help for it. Show him in, and set another place beside me."

The nameless man bowed and hurried away as Dominic reached over to take her hand. Melissa forced herself not to recoil.

"My apologies, my dear, but it looks like your night is about to get worse."

*Worse than being kidnapped by monsters able to control my every move?* she wanted to snap.

"What do you mean?" she asked instead.

"You're in for a bit of a shock I'd imagine." He patted her hand.

*Shock?* But the double doors at the end of the room were already opening.

A man strode forward, his face shadowed by the darker hall. When he stepped into the light, however, Melissa pushed to her feet, her jaw dropping.

"No," she breathed.

Tarian stopped at the foot of the table, staring back at her with eyes as cold as ice.

# Chapter Six

People were speaking all around her. The low buzz in her ears was proof of that. They didn't matter, though. Not her captors or their mad leader. All that mattered was that Tarian had walked into a room full of necromancers.

Necromancers who didn't seem surprised to see him.

There was no expression on Tarian's face as he waited for her to come to grips with her new reality. Her brain felt frozen, her thoughts sluggish. She didn't know how to process the idea of Tarian standing in this pit of vipers.

And when she did, she wished she hadn't.

He was a necromancer. He'd known her from the first moment they'd met, and his people had been looking for a high profile vampire to use as leverage. How easy it must have been to flirt with her, a lonely vampire willing to jump at any chance that presented itself.

The pieces of this tragic puzzle fit together one after another. His resistance to the idea of a night spent in her apartment, instead of at a restaurant, made perfect sense. Changing locations would have screwed up her abduction.

What made everything worse was the realization that his "gentlemanly behavior" had probably been one more strategic act. He was her enemy. The odds that he'd actually wanted her were slim, but stringing her along had been a good way to ensure he'd be able to maneuver her as he wished while he waited for his chance to strike. Shame sliced through her. Here she'd been plotting to get him into bed and he'd neatly sidestepped her every attempt. The passion in his kiss had all been artifice. No one could touch a lover the way he had and then hand them over to kidnappers if their feelings had been even remotely engaged.

Which meant every word, every caress, had been a lie. He'd played her and she'd fallen for every bit of it.

Her eyes closed, blocking out the sight of him. Her father had warned her. She should have listened. Now she found that one of the last people to see her before her abduction was part of the scheme. Would her family ever track her down? Even for Lucian it'd be an impossible feat.

The hope that someone would be able to find her flickered and died in her chest. No doubt Tarian had already been questioned. It'd be child's play for him to send the investigation in the wrong direction.

Resolve filled her, banishing the pain ripping her apart. When she opened her eyes she did not look at Tarian with the longing of a lover but the clear gaze of an adversary. Every person on this property was her enemy, and she'd best them all. She didn't need someone to rescue her. She'd do it herself.

Somehow.

Tarian moved forward, though his eyes never left hers. Rounding the table, he crossed the length of the room to Dominic's side.

"Grandfather," he said with a bow.

Melissa didn't even flinch at the word. His relationship with her captor was irrelevant. It was just one more piece of proof that all she'd been to him was a means to an end.

"How did you find us?" Dominic said, gesturing to the chair that had been brought for Tarian.

"Eilin," he replied as he sat. "You should have told me yourself."

"I didn't think you'd have the stomach for such business."

Tarian reached for the roll on Dominic's plate. "It's been a long time since we've spoken. You don't know what I have the stomach for anymore."

"You've left your pacifist ways behind you then?" Dominic passed him the butter as if his sudden appearance was the most normal thing in the world.

"Of course." Tarian sliced open his roll. "They were the ideals of a foolish young man. I can see this new world we're in, Grandfather. The vampires need to be reminded they fear us for a reason."

Dominic clapped a hand on his shoulder. "I can't tell you how good it is to hear that, Tarian."

He took a bite of the roll before saying, "You should have brought me in on this."

"Apologies. Even leaders make mistakes. But you played your part all the same. Without you we never would have had access to the Redgrave."

Both men turned to her, but she kept her face carefully blank.

"Melissa, I realize you may have lost your appetite," Dominic said solicitously. "But you need to keep up your strength. Drink."

Again her body moved without her permission, raising the glass to her lips. Beneath the table, she fisted her hand in fury. It seemed a hundred times worse being treated as a puppet in front of Tarian. Was he enjoying her humiliation?

She risked a glance at him in time to see a tiny frown mar his face before it smoothed into bland amusement.

"She is easy to control," Dominic said with all the interest one would show a lab rat. "Given her relatively young age it should be a simple matter to confine her to the house."

"Excellent," Tarian replied. "Perhaps the children can practice on her."

"Terrific idea. I'll see to it a session is arranged for tomorrow. We'll need every member of our community in the best shape possible in case things go wrong with the vampires."

Tarian gestured to one of the waiting servers to fill his plate. "They may outnumber us but our powers are stronger than they believe. It would be unwise for them to attack directly."

"I doubt it will come to that. Lucian is a reasonable man and say what you want about the vampire, he loves his family." Dominic reached out to stroke her cheek. Melissa quelled the urge to sink her teeth into his hand. "He'll want this lovely creature back."

"When will you send the ransom demand?" Tarian asked, cutting a piece of chicken.

"I thought I'd let them stew for a day or two. Once they are truly panicked they'll be more inclined to consider our offer."

"Wise." He ate without so much as glancing in her direction. The irony that they'd shared their last meal together laughing and flirting didn't escape her. What a difference a day made.

Grabbing her wine glass of her own accord she drained the last drops.

"Dominic," she said, setting the glass down. "If you were speaking truthfully about allowing me to walk around this house freely, then I'd like to be excused. Recent company is turning my stomach."

Though the smile never left Dominic's face, she saw anger flash through his eyes. Perhaps she should have resisted the urge to comment on Tarian.

However, Dominic merely patted her hand. "Of course, my dear," he said. "You remember the way to your room."

"Yes." She tossed her napkin onto the table and stood. Not bothering to look at her betrayer, she stalked from the room with her head held high.

The second the doors to the dining room closed behind her, she collapsed against the wall. Out, she needed out.

Calling on her vampire super speed she raced to the window, only to see armed guards patrolling the perimeter of the property. She retraced her steps to the front hall to find another guard in black posted at the door. He looked at her with dead eyes as if daring her to try something.

*Caged in,* she thought.

Abandoning the obvious exits, she raced up the stairs to the second floor. She searched through all the guest bedrooms but no window was free of bars, though thankfully it seemed only her room was rigged with twenty-four hour monitoring. On top of that dilemma was the added problem that no room held weapons of any sort. All she was able to find was a silver letter opener in what looked like one of the necromancer's private rooms.

"Damn," she breathed, looking down at the metal that would severely burn her. She'd have to wrap it in something.

Fangs lengthened in her mouth as she walked to the long gray curtains. Grabbing the material, she tore a strip off the bottom with her teeth.

It wasn't terribly thick, but it would do the job. Carefully she draped the cloth over the letter opener. Though her hand tingled uncomfortably, her palm didn't blister when she picked up the blade.

Melissa raced back to her room, thankful not to cross paths with one of the guards. Her black dress didn't leave many places to hide a weapon. Upon entering her room, she was careful to block the camera's view of her treasure until she was able to safely store it under her pillow.

Her brief spurt of victory was short lived, however, when the reality of her situation crashed back to her. One weapon that she could barely hold wouldn't get her out of a compound this well locked down.

She needed a plan and fast. Because everything she'd seen so far made it impossible to imagine a successful escape on her own.

And she was, without a doubt, alone.

• • •

Rage churned within Tarian as he pasted a smile on his face and ate his dinner as if nothing out of the ordinary had happened.

"Was Melissa always your target?" he asked, choking down his food.

"We had a short list of candidates," Dominic replied. "But she made the most sense. When Eilin called about your date, we had our chance. She'd be away from the office with its advanced security, and the odds of her taking guards on a date were slim."

"What did you do to her driver?"

Dominic waved his hand. "A casualty of war, I'm afraid."

"I trust Lucian won't find the body anytime soon."

"Burned up in the dawn," Dominic said. "But you know what was interesting? The vampire had a rield on her wrist."

Tarian kept his face carefully blank. "Really? How is that possible?"

There was no denying the sharp intelligence in his grandfather's eyes. "She said her father gave it to her."

Relief spiraled through him, though he had little doubt Melissa's instincts to protect him had ended the moment he'd walked into this room "It's possible," he mused. "We should look into how he acquired one. Was it a lucky purchase, or does he have a necromancer captive who made it?"

"A good point," Dominic said. "But any necromancer strong enough to make a rield would be very hard to capture."

"True."

"Still, it is in our best interest to discover the rield's origins just in case."

"It must have been difficult to capture her without using necromancer magic," Tarian said.

"I always plan ahead," Dominic replied. "We had some deadman's thistle ready, but the leech still put up a fight. Jamie has a set of claw marks across his chest that can attest to the battle."

*Good girl*, Tarian thought, giving in to a moment of bloodlust. He'd known Melissa was strong. "He'll recover I trust," he said, keeping up his facade.

"Yes, but it's fortunate you are here. We could use an extra set of hands to replace him while he heals."

"Whatever you require, Grandfather. I'm here to help."

Dominic smiled as his plate was cleared away. "We'll be on a nocturnal schedule for the duration of the vampire's confinement. To ensure she is always watched, of course. We'll drug her through the daylight hours."

"She's barely a century old," Tarian replied. "I doubt she's able to keep her eyes open during the day."

"Even so. Better safe than sorry."

"As you wish." Tarian paused, weighing his options. He mustn't look too eager to interact with Melissa or suspicion would be raised. Still, an opportunity was an opportunity. "Do you drug her by drink or injection?"

"Drink," Dominic replied. "With only a small glass of blood for dinner, she'll be hungry by the early hours of the morning. We might not even have to force her to drink."

"Allow me," Tarian said. "It would give me a certain satisfaction to bend the vampire to my wishes."

Dominic sipped his wine, studying Tarian as he did so. "Have a soft spot for her, do you?"

Tarian laughed derisively. "For a leech? The world would be a better place if they were wiped from existence."

"And yet you were attempting to date her."

He shrugged. "I am serious about finding a mate, and our dinner was set up by the agency I joined. Besides, I was curious. To be that close to a Redgrave, to toy with her as one would a mouse…" Tarian smiled and knew it wasn't a comforting expression. "What an opportunity."

"What would have become of it had we not kidnapped the girl?"

He set down his cutlery on the empty plate. "I would have enjoyed playing with her. I couldn't have revealed myself, you understand, but there'd be some vindication in breaking her heart."

"How cold. I wouldn't have thought you capable of such calculated cruelty."

"I've never forgotten what killed my father," he replied, truth coloring his words. "The vampires owe me."

Dominic clapped a hand on his shoulder. "That they do, my boy. Take the leech her blood. Wring whatever satisfaction you can out of her, but remember, we need her in one piece to negotiate with."

"I'll control myself," he promised. He didn't know what Dominic read in his face, but it put a wide smile on his grandfather's lips.

"Good to have you onboard," Dominic said.

The approval in the older man's eyes turned his stomach. All the years he'd spent avoiding this man hadn't been wasted.

But he had someone to protect now. And somehow, he had to sneak a vampire out of a full house of necromancers, without anyone realizing what he was about until it was too late.

# Chapter Seven

Dawn was coming. She could feel her energy draining and struggled to keep her eyes open. The day would make her more vulnerable than she could afford to be. Dominic could walk in and stake her, and there wouldn't be a damn thing she could do about it.

Her stomach rumbled as she paced the confines of her bedroom. The necromancers had left her alone in the hours since dinner, and for that, at least, she was grateful. She'd spent that time trying to think of any way out of her predicament but had yet to come up with a viable plan.

A knock sounded at the door. Drawing on her vampire speed she raced to the bed as the door opened. If she had to go for the letter opener, she wanted to be close enough to reach it.

Tarian stepped into the room before closing the door behind him.

Again her heart lurched at the sight of him. It wasn't fair

that she knew what he was but her body's reaction was unchanged. There was nothing good about this man. He wasn't the mate she'd been waiting for. He was just a manipulative bastard.

"What are you doing here?"

"I brought you a snack." He held up a glass of blood.

Her stomach twisted at the temptation, but she shook her head. "I'm not hungry."

"Liar."

He walked closer to her, and her eyes flicked to the camera above the door. As always, the red light indicating its power was glowing brightly.

*Don't attack unless you have to,* she reasoned. Dominic could be watching her every move.

"I'm sure you must be feeling exhausted after your ordeal," Tarian said, his face blank. "A few sips and you'll feel better."

"As if you care about my comfort, necromancer," she hissed. "Every word between us was a lie."

"Of course," he replied. "It was most amusing to see how easy it was to wrap you around my finger. A little affection and you were ready to do anything I wanted. No magic needed."

*Don't slap him,* she ordered herself. *Don't rise to his bait.*

"I hate you," she said instead, honesty dripping from her words.

His smile slipped. "I know."

She waited for another taunt, but he said nothing. Melissa frowned. What was he waiting for?

"Why did you bring me blood?" she asked.

"Dinner wasn't enough to keep you going. Aren't you

hungry?"

She wasn't a fool. Not anymore. "It's unnecessary to drug me when I'll be helpless once the sun comes up anyway."

He held up his hands in the universal you-got-me signal. "I confess this blood might be spiked, but we both know you'll drink it one way or the other. Don't make this harder than it has to be."

She shifted backward. "As far as you are concerned, the hard way is the only option on the table."

Instead of sending his power to flow over her, however, he only waited.

"What are you doing?" she demanded. His words were what she expected from an enemy, but his actions were not. He made no move to force her. He didn't even bother getting too close.

It was she who took a step forward, studying his face.

Something wasn't what it seemed.

A tiny click, only audible to immortal ears, sounded in the quiet room, and they both turned to see the red camera light switch off.

*Free*, she thought, ready to take advantage of the camera malfunction. She might not be able to escape, but at least she could take her pound of flesh without Dominic calling in backup.

Flying to the bed, she grabbed the silver letter opener even as she heard Tarian call out.

Fire flashed up her arm when her fingers touched the cursed metal, but she didn't pause. Whirling around, she drove the blade toward Tarian's chest.

The glass of blood smashed to the floor as Tarian blocked her attack and neatly twisted the letter opener from her hand.

"No," she cried as the burning metal fell to the ground. It had been her one chance. The only time she could hurt him the way he had her.

Tarian didn't even glance at the fallen weapon; instead he grabbed her wrist and forced her hand up to his view. Burns blistered her fingers, and angry red welts littered her palm.

"What did you do?" he breathed.

"Let go of me, you monster," she snarled, tugging at her hand.

But he didn't let her go. Bending low, he pressed his lips to the unharmed skin of her wrist.

Melissa blinked, looking down at his bent head. "What new game is this?"

"No game," he said, rising. "We need to get you out of here as soon as possible."

Hope tugged at her before she forced it back. "You're lying," she reasoned. "This is some new trick, and I'm not playing."

Tarian grabbed her arms, giving her a shake. "Listen to me. I only rigged the camera to give us a brief window of opportunity. We need to leave while we have the chance."

She studied his face and saw only honesty. "I don't understand."

"Dominic's plan will set both our races on a collision course. I'm trying to stop a war. Help me do that."

"What do you care?"

His hands tightened on her. "My people will die, just as easily as yours, if you stay in my grandfather's clutches. I'll take you back to New York, Melissa, but you have to trust me."

"Sure. Hell should be freezing over any day now." She tore herself from his grip.

Tarian ran a hand through his hair. "Fine, but you want out of here as much as I do. I'm your ticket, sweetheart. Make your choice."

Melissa glanced at the deactivated camera. Dare she believe him? If it was a trick, she wouldn't be any worse off than she was now, just a bit more humiliated, and that was survivable.

But if he was telling the truth…

"I don't trust you," she said. "I do, however, need you."

"Good enough." He held out his hand.

She hesitated before slipping her uninjured hand into his.

"Let's go." He tugged her out the door.

The hall was empty as they crept toward the stairs.

"This is insane," she whispered.

"Most people are asleep," he replied. "The whole night schedule thing is not a popular decision."

"I'm betting the guards aren't asleep."

"Luckily, there's a distraction in the back of the house."

Melissa glanced at him and saw the utter concentration on his face. Maybe this wasn't a prank after all.

They raced down the staircase, hopping over the one creaky step. The guard at the front door was absent, and Melissa ran forward across the entryway.

"Careful," Tarian said, pulling her back when she would have grabbed the door. "Give me a minute."

Opening the door, he stepped out into the pre-dawn morning.

Melissa pressed against the wall as she listened to Tarian call out to the guards in the front yard.

"There's smoke billowing from the kitchen," he said, his voice filled with urgency. "Dominic wants all hands on deck."

"We can't leave our posts," one guard argued.

"If we don't stop a fire, there won't be posts to worry about. I drugged the vampire myself, so there's no danger of escape. Why else do you think Dominic would have sent me?"

"I see smoke rising over the house," one called.

Melissa arched a brow. What had Tarian done?

"You three go help. I'll man the front door," an authoritative guard ordered.

Footsteps ran passed the door as Melissa slid further along the hall wall in case she was spotted.

"I'll stand guard," Tarian said. "Go help my grandfather."

"I'm not leaving this position unless Dominic himself orders me gone."

There was a pause before magic began to seep through the air. Melissa shivered, rubbing her hands along her arms for warmth.

"Dominic is requesting you," Tarian said, but something was off about his voice.

Inching closer to the door, Melissa dared a small glance around the corner.

The guard stood transfixed, staring at Tarian with a blank expression.

"You will go and help the others. If anyone asks, another guard is holding the door."

"Another guard is here," he said, swaying slightly.

"Good man," Tarian purred. "Now go. It's an emergency.

Run."

The guard took off at a hard sprint.

Melissa ducked back behind the door as Tarian turned. What had she just witnessed? Necromancers couldn't command each other the way they could vampires. What had Tarian done?

But before she had time to puzzle out the strange occurrence, Tarian popped around the door.

"Come." He held out his hand.

*Better the devil you know*, she reasoned, joining him.

He pulled her out into the yard as they ran for the cars parked in the driveway.

"Please tell me one of these is yours," she said.

He already had the keys in his hand. She spotted one car's lights flash as Tarian pressed the button on his fob with a beep.

She slid into the passenger's seat as he jumped behind the wheel. With a turn of the keys, the engine roared to life.

"Hang on," he said, wheeling them around.

Melissa bit back a cry as they reversed into another car before Tarian stomped the gas. Grabbing for the door handle, she held on tight as they shot forward across the flat desert landscape.

"We're going to be pretty easy to spot," she said as the speedometer climbed above a hundred.

"The kitchen will keep them busy for a few minutes, and I've got a recording of you lying down set to play on a loop when the cameras switch back on. We should have at least a bit of time to put distance between them and us."

"Did you go all *Firestarter* on the house or something?"

"It's just a very small, contained fire," he replied.

"External damage only, nothing that will harm the structure of the building. My goal is to save lives, not endanger them."

She twisted on the seat to face him. "You better start explaining what the hell is going on, or I will be introducing you to my claws and stealing this car."

"Try."

Fangs exploded in her mouth as she hissed at him. "I am not playing."

"Neither am I," he shot back. "Nothing about this situation warrants humor of any kind."

"Who are you?"

"I already told you that. I wasn't lying when we met."

She scoffed. "I beg to differ. I think several rather vital facts were left out of our initial conversations."

His fingers tapped against the steering wheel. "Nothing I say right now will make you any less angry at me. Just trust that I had nothing to do with your kidnapping."

"Right. Date a necromancer and then get abducted by a whole group of them. Total coincidence."

"As incredible as it seems, I don't walk around with criminal intentions, just waiting for the perfect opportunity to strike."

"Well, aren't you one of a kind."

She saw his jaw clench tight enough to make a vein throb in his temple. "You have an ignorant view of my people."

"Given the current situation, I think my belief in the danger of necromancers is pretty damn valid."

"One group," he stressed. "One small faction of radicals. They do not speak for the entire population."

"Yes, because the rest of you are cuddly teddy bears. Must have been a different race that laid waste to half of

Europe during the necromancer wars."

"My only point is, not every one of us is evil," he said. "I came to rescue you, didn't I?"

Melissa leaned back against the car door, her body angled to face him. "So you weren't pursuing me with evil intent?"

He glanced at her before turning back to the road. "No."

"Then why…"

"What is the point of defending myself, Melissa?" he cut her off. "You already think I'm a monster, along with the rest of my people."

She didn't deny his words, and her silence only caused him to grip the steering wheel tighter.

"Tell me how this plays out for you, necromancer. You can't imagine my people will welcome your return to the city with open arms."

"Luckily, I have days to convince you to be my champion."

Melissa snorted. "Not bloody likely. I'm getting on the first plane I can find."

"You'll never reach New York," he replied. "My grandfather is a powerful man. Necromancers will either catch you boarding or disembarking. Hell, they might hijack the whole damn plane. They've shown their hand with your abduction. No turning back now. They have to recover you at all costs. Air travel is not an option."

Dread filled her. He wasn't wrong. The race was now to see if she could reach New York before the necromancers reached her.

"I'm sure you're about to offer a plan that's not in the least bit self-serving."

"We drive," he said shortly. "We use cash, and we stay as

far off the beaten path as possible."

"With you." There was no doubting the disdain in her voice.

Tarian glanced at her then back to the road. "Right now, Melissa, I don't care if you hate me. This is far bigger than you or I. All you need to focus on is getting back to your father, and I can help you do it."

She tapped her fingers on the door handle as she considered her options. Though she didn't have her purse or credit cards, she could surely beg a phone call from someone. Her father had contacts all over the country. There must be somewhere safe she could go.

Her next move, however, was the least of her current problems.

"I'm going to put a pin in this argument for the moment," she said, trying to keep herself calm. "Because dawn in coming."

She held out her hand to show small wisps of smoke curling from her fingers.

Tarian swore as he swerved onto the side of the road. "Get out," he ordered, jumping from the car.

Melissa pushed free of her seat just as the sun broke over the horizon. A cry tore from her as light hit her body. Agony flared in every cell in her body as her skin started to blister. Full-on flames were only moments away.

But then Tarian was there at her side, ushering her toward the open trunk. He lifted her in and shrugged out of his jacket.

"It's not perfect, but it will keep you protected while I find somewhere to stay for the day," he said, throwing the jacket over her head.

Melissa heard the trunk slam shut, encasing her in near darkness. The collision from their escape, however, must have warped the trunk's seal. She scuttled back as far as she could to avoid the thin strips of sunlight streaming through gaps. When she woke she'd have some serious blisters to heal, but at least she'd survive.

At least, as long as Tarian didn't wait till high noon and open the trunk to roast her alive.

*He risked a lot to free me,* she reasoned. *I'm valuable to him alive.*

But in the end it made no difference whether she could trust him or not. Dawn was fully upon her, and she lost her struggle to keep her eyes open.

As she slipped into her daylight sleep, she prayed Tarian would find some way to keep her safe from the merciless sun.

# Chapter Eight

She opened her eyes to the water stained ceiling of a cheap motel. Turning her head, Melissa saw Tarian lying next to her, sound asleep. One arm was thrown over her waist, and she wasn't sure whether it was to keep tabs on her or just an unconscious caress.

Moving slowly so as not to disturb him, she twisted her head to scan the room. It had been many years since she'd been in such a run-down motel. She wouldn't be surprised if she'd seen it as the setting in a horror movie.

The yellow walls and wood paneling had a distinctive seventies vibe, as did the beaten down forest green carpet. A television with old rabbit-ear antennas perched atop the one set of drawers, but she could see its electrical cord had been chewed through by some small creature.

Tarian had wisely stripped the bed of the ugly floral bedspread which likely hadn't seen the inside of a washing machine in months. The only light came from the single bare bulb set in the center of a slowly rotating beige fan. All in all, the room wasn't worth whatever fee Tarian had paid for it. And that was absolutely perfect. No one would ever imagine an heiress to bed down in a place like this.

Turning back to her bed partner, she wondered what her next move should be. She might be able to use her super speed to run from the room before Tarian woke enough to trap her with his magic. Once on her own, however, was she better off or worse? She didn't know this part of the country, but Tarian obviously did. If she could reach a phone and contact her father, backup would be sent her way, but it would still take time to reach her—time where she'd be vulnerable.

Of course, choosing a necromancer as a traveling companion came with its own host of pitfalls.

*Better on my own,* she decided. At least if she failed, it would be due to her own choices, not because she was naïve enough to trust an enemy.

Melissa eyed the door, knowing she'd only have one chance. She'd have to be fast. Faster than she'd ever been before.

Behind her Tarian inhaled as his body started to wake, and she shot from the bed.

She was out of the room and flying down the corridor in seconds. Decreasing room numbers flashed passed her as she sprinted for the stairs. Her vampire speed allowed her to cross the distance in a fraction of the time it would take a human.

The stairwell was only a few feet in front of her when magic washed over her skin

*No,* she thought as her legs stopped running.

She jerked to a halt, standing frozen in the motel hallway. Without her permission, her body turned, and she saw Tarian leaning against the doorjamb of their room. He hadn't even bothered to chase after her. Not that he'd need to.

With his powers surrounding her, her feet moved forward of their own accord as she walked back to her betrayer. Unlike when Dominic had controlled her, Tarian's magic wasn't biting. It caressed her skin in a touch that was unwelcome but not wholly unpleasant. The fear she'd felt when Dominic had controlled her was absent under his command.

*You're a fool*, she told herself. He posed just as great a threat to her as his grandfather. The fact that he could use his magic on her without a qualm was proof of that.

Her legs stopped moving when it reached the door to their room.

"I'm going to release you," Tarian said, arms crossed over his chest. "It's your choice whether to walk into this room so we can have a civilized conversation or whether I have to chase you down again."

The tingling in her limbs drained away, until she was once again in control.

"I'm going to enjoy watching my father eviscerate you," she promised with a smile.

"Let's just add this to the list of things I need to make up to you before we reach New York." He gestured into the room, and she strode passed him with her head held high. The last thing she wanted him to know was how unnerved she was to be powerless in his presence.

Melissa heard the door close behind her but refused to turn. Instead, she went to the window and looked out at the dark parking lot. She wasn't used to being the weaker partner in any sort of relationship. Vampires were stronger than most immortals, but all her usual advantages were wiped away with Tarian. She had nothing to fight with if things went south, and the knowledge made her want to do physical damage.

"This isn't how I wanted to start our night," he said from behind her.

"I can't tell you how devastated I am to have ruined your plans."

"Let's have a seat and discuss our situation calmly."

"Or, and I'm just tossing ideas around here, I could continue to curse the day you walked into my life and do everything in my power to escape you." She turned, ready to stare him down. "Decisions, decisions."

"You could," he agreed, as he perched on the edge of the bed. "But you'll fail."

Her fangs burst from her gums as she hissed at him. "If at first you don't succeed—"

"You don't want to try again."

Silence stretched as she regarded the man she'd been so happy to see walk into her office just a few nights ago. Now everything was different. Her world was splintering and she had no idea who to trust.

"Is this were we get to the portion of the evening where you rain threats down on me?" she murmured.

His eyes were blank as he looked at her. No hint of her boyish would-be lover remained in the necromancer before her.

"That's not how I want this to play out," he replied.

"But a bastard's gotta do what a bastard's gotta do, am I right?"

He stood, and every instinct in her flared to life, even though he looked harmless enough.

"I don't want to use my power on you. Never did. I regret that circumstances made it necessary to do so today."

"Please," she replied. "Necromancers love nothing more than to use vampires like puppets."

"I've told you before, you have no concept of my race."

A smile twisted her lips but she doubted her expression was pleasant. "Your grandfather gave me a crash course."

"We're nothing alike."

"I'm sure."

"I gave you a rield."

The words cut off the snarky comment she'd been about to voice. Instead she kept her peace and waited for him to continue.

"Dominic took it from you, so I know you understand what it means."

She swallowed before inclining her head. "I don't know why you gave it to me, though."

"I wanted to protect you," he replied, walking toward her. "Even from myself."

"Out of character."

He shook his head. "Had we worked out, I never wanted you to doubt, even for a moment, that all your decisions had been your own."

Her heart twisted in her chest.

"I've told you before, but I'll say it again." He stopped before her. "You'll always be safe with me."

Her breath caught. Sincerity infused the simple vow. It was far too tempting to believe him, to step into his arms and let the world fall away. Even knowing what he was, she didn't want to be his enemy.

Tarian reached for her before his hand paused and eventually dropped. "What I am doesn't define who I am," he said.

"Make me another bracelet, and I'll consider believing you," she offered. "Prove you won't control me and then maybe…" She let the words trail off, not knowing what she could promise.

Tarian shook his head. "I can't."

"Why?"

"Making a rield requires time and resources, neither of which we have available. It also requires a deep store of power. I won't be able to make another one for years."

She blinked. Though Dominic had been shocked to see the bracelet on her, she hadn't thought it was an item of such priceless value.

"What if you'd met your mate in the next few years, and I was still wearing the only rield you could create?" she whispered.

Tarian looked away, refusing to answer the question.

Confusion swept through her mind. Had she been a fleeting tryst, he wouldn't have wasted the gift on her. Which meant he'd either intended to get it back or…

Or he'd been serious about thinking of her as a potential mate.

She shook her head to try and find some clarity.

"Answer me this, then. If you had a rield in your possession right now, would you give it to me?"

Tarian exhaled slowly before turning back to her. The sincerity and regret that had filled his face were gone, replaced with an enigmatic mask.

"No," he said. "When we first met, I was trying to be noble. Now I'm trying to stop a war."

"And you'll do whatever it takes to achieve that goal."

"Yes."

"Monster."

His hands shot out to grip her arms at the soft charge.

"I'm trying to save more than just necromancer lives."

"So you say."

She lifted her chin and met his gaze, even though her instincts urged her to yield. Tarian held all the cards. She should be trying to appease him instead of pushing him to react. No matter what her circumstances, however, she didn't have it in her to back down. Not even before a necromancer who watched her with barely concealed anger burning in his eyes.

He pushed her back against the wall as he crowded into her space.

"You're trying my patience."

"If I had a nickel."

His hands tightened on her arms. "You will accompany me to New York, even if I have to enspell you across the whole damn country."

Looked like her dashing would-be mate had no qualms about forcing her to behave like a doll whenever she proved a little less malleable than he wished. Good to know. Not the least bit devastating at all.

"Then I guess I'll learn exactly what kind of man you are."

All emotion, even the anger, was wiped clean from his face. Ice slithered down her spine as she looked into the blank blue eyes regarding her. Despite her bravado, she did not want this man in her head.

"I'm backed into a corner," he said. "And I'll do anything to avert this coming disaster."

"Why do you need me?" she demanded. "Just let me go, Tarian."

He gave a sharp shake of his head.

"Your father will rip apart my people when he discovers Dominic was behind your abduction."

"True."

"That means we have one chance of stopping this before it gets out of hand. Necromancers took you, so necromancers need to return you. You've got to end up in New York with me as a sign of good faith so we can convince Redgrave not all of us are evil."

"First you've got to convince me."

"I'm always up for a challenge."

Options flew through her mind. Strike out on her own, try to contact Lucian, stay with Tarian. She had no idea which choice would help her most.

"Melissa," Tarian said, a thread of warmth creeping back into his voice. "Your chances of survival are slim on your own." His grip tightened on her as he added, "And mine are non-existent without you."

"I should care what happens to you?"

He didn't flinch, she'd give him that. "I have a sister to protect," he said. "Not to mention a whole race your people could annihilate. You can hate me, Melissa, but I'm not leaving you until New York."

"And if I decided not to ally myself with my enemy, you'll make the choice for me."

Tarian shook his head. "Don't ask me to choose between

you and my entire race."

Because she'd lose. Whatever they had in New York, obviously it hadn't meant to him what it had to her.

"Fine. Whatever you say. It's not like I have a choice in the matter."

He didn't move. "Give me your word you won't try and escape me. Do it, and I'll swear not to use my powers on you."

She inhaled out of habit at the unexpected offer. His powers were his trump card. Never before had she encountered an enemy willing to give up his advantage so easily.

"Why?" she demanded. What sort of trick was he pulling?

"Because despite what you believe, I never wanted to use them on you in the first place. It's a promise I'll be happy to make."

"No power. Not ever. I don't care what situation we get into, I stay with you, and you keep your creepy magic off me."

"That's the deal."

She chewed her lip as she mulled over her options. There was no denying it was the best deal she could hope to wring from him. Not to mention, given the circumstances, it might not be a bad idea to stick together. Though a phone call would have her father's men to her in hours, Tarian was right. There would be no hiding such a public rescue, and the vampires would consider this an attack on their race. They'd lose any chance at avoiding conflict, and the resulting uprising would put vampire lives in jeopardy. Her immediate safety was not worth igniting a war. Taking a road trip with a necromancer, however, didn't exactly sound like her kind of vacation.

"If you break your word, I will never trust you again," she cautioned. "I don't care what sort of partnership we build. You use your magic on me, and we are through."

"You don't trust me now."

"You know what I mean."

He inclined his head. "I will keep my promise."

Melissa exhaled slowly before she made her decision. "Deal. I'll stay with you. But if you betray me, I'll use all of my father's considerable resources to hunt you down and make you regret it."

"Duly noted."

Pushing him back, she jerked away from his grip and paced the length of the room. "How long will it take to drive back to the city?"

"Forty hours, give or take," he replied. "You didn't do too well in the trunk, though, so I'd suggest only traveling at night."

"Four nights or so," she said, factoring in the average hours of darkness. She could stand his company for that long, especially if she'd either be unconscious or behind the wheel most of that time.

"Fine," she said. "Then we should get on the road as soon as possible."

"Ready when you are."

Melissa smoothed a hand down her dress, noting the scorch marks where the sun had burned her skin. Several red welts still showed on her calves, but most of her daylight injuries were well on their way to healing.

"I've got to stop somewhere to change," she said. "I know the heroines in adventure movies might run from exploding buildings in tight dresses and stiletto heels, but in reality we do better with jeans and running shoes."

Tarian gestured to the broken down chair in the corner. A gray Wal-Mart bag waited for her.

"I thought of that," he said. "Once you were settled in, I did a quick run."

She took the bag and refrained from thanking him for the unexpected thoughtfulness.

"I had to guess at the sizes," he replied, striding back to the bed.

"I'm sure they'll be fine," she said and slipped into the bathroom.

There she traded her Dior dress and Jimmy Choos for polyester and sneakers. Glancing in the mirror, she saw every trace of a curl had left her hair, and her makeup had more or less vanished. She looked…ordinary. Something she hadn't been since her human days.

*You're a Redgrave,* she told herself. *The match of any necromancer, no matter how old.*

Rolling her shoulders back, she lifted her chin. In four nights she'd be home. She could do this. As long as she remembered the real Tarian was the one who had forcibly brought her back to this room, not the one who had shown up at her office with lunch and even more delicious kisses. Whatever reason he'd had for pursuing her, she bet it wasn't because of her awesome dating abilities. Which meant she had to keep her foolish, romantic heart firmly in check. She might have deluded herself into thinking he was the man of her dreams, but she'd never been the woman of his.

Opening the door, she found Tarian standing with his back to her. She paused and took the opportunity to study him. Tension knotted in his tight shoulders. He must have had time to exchange his regular suits for more casual attire before setting out after her but still, she appreciated the speed at which he'd managed to come to her aid.

*You're a means to an end to him,* she told herself. *Even if that end is in everyone's best interests. It doesn't change the facts.*

She couldn't trust him. Ever.

"I'm ready," she called.

He turned to her, but there was no pleasure in his eyes. "Then we should get going."

"I'll drive," she offered. "You couldn't have gotten much sleep."

He inclined his head. The fact that he hadn't argued told her just how exhausted he must be. She'd slept the day away while he'd put a safe buffer between them and Dominic. Given that he'd spent the night before awake with the necromancers, he must be asleep on his feet.

Together they left the run down motel in wary harmony.

She couldn't remember the last time she'd had to drive herself anywhere. Not only was Manhattan not exactly conducive to owning a car, but she had a driver whenever there was a need. Ignoring the whole trying-to-avoid-a-group-of-zealous-necromancers thing, she rather enjoyed the freedom of the wide open Arizona roads. While Tarian slept in the passenger seat, she'd spent hours flying down the dark pavement. There was definitely something to be said for racing through the desert on empty roads, feeling like the last people on earth.

However, her joy at the open road shriveled when her companion came to. Melissa glanced at the clock on the dashboard, wondering if she could use the dawn as an excuse to pull over for the night and escape the confines of the small car. But the traitorous timepiece showed at least two hours before she could justify stopping for the day.

"No trouble?" Tarian asked, pushing himself up in the seat.

"No sign of your criminal cousins," she replied. "Looks like we're still ahead of them."

Silence stretched, and it was anything but comfortable.

"You made good time tonight," he offered, glancing out the window.

"Not like there are many cops to catch me in these parts."

"If we continue to make such speed we might shave a few hours off our estimate."

Her hands tightened on the steering wheel. "Excellent news."

"Still, it's good to know that—"

"Stop," Melissa cut in. "Just...stop." She drew in a deep breath out of habit as she tried to figure out how to best phrase her request. "I can't sit here and chitchat with you as if nothing has happened," she said.

His head turned slowly to look at her. His powers might allow him to sense the changes in her body, but that advantage worked both ways. Melissa counted the steady heartbeats echoing in her ears.

"I regret you were drawn into this." His words broke the uncomfortable silence.

She glanced at him before looking back at the road. "Your fault."

"I know."

"What, did you walk into Fated Match and decide it was a great day to screw with a vampire's life?"

"No."

"Was I your way of taking your pound of flesh from the vamp community?"

"Didn't even cross my mind."

Her grip on the steering wheel tightened. Those words had sounded so sincere, and the weakest part of her wished they were. "Then why?" she said. "Why did you pursue me?"

His gaze never wavered from her. Melissa felt its weight like a physical touch as she waited for him to respond.

"You won't believe a thing I say," he told her, his voice soft in the quiet of the car. "Any answer I offer will be dismissed. Tell me I'm wrong."

What had she expected? That he start waxing poetically about being struck by her beauty and just having to have her, despite the barrier of their species? Her life rarely worked out so perfectly. No, there was more to the story than lust, if he'd even been serious about his attraction to her.

*He's right.* She'd distrust whatever answer he gave her. It was a useless line of inquiry. Melissa shook her head, knowing just days ago she would have trusted him so easily because she'd foolishly hoped he was something he could never be.

"There's a twenty-four hour convenience store ahead," she said, as they drove through one of the small towns that had peppered their journey. "We should stop for supplies."

She didn't bother waiting for his reply, merely slowed to

a halt outside the brightly lit store. Pushing from the car, she inhaled the desert night air. She needed a break. Trying to figure Tarian out was giving her a headache.

As she walked up the wooden steps to the store, she tried to run her hand through her hair only to have her fingers get stuck in the tangles. Looked like stopping would serve two purposes. She could catch her breath, figuratively, and get a hairbrush all in one fell swoop.

A tiny bell chimed as she entered the store. Rows of shelves, housing every item you never knew you desperately needed, waited before her. The cashier barely cast her a glance before turning back to the small TV perched before him.

Melissa grabbed a wire basket and stepped into the aisles. She heard the chime indicating Tarian had joined her but didn't bother to glance back. Instead she wandered further, looking over the bags of chips and bottles of pop she couldn't consume.

Moving to the toiletry section, she threw a hairbrush and a pack of elastic ties into her basket. An overpriced stick of deodorant followed as did two toothbrushes. Though their last room had provided them, she didn't know if that trend would hold for the next place they stayed.

Rounding the row, she saw Tarian tossing bottles of water and power bars into his basket. The sight reminded her that while her companion could refuel with relative ease, she could not.

*Problem for another time,* she thought, pushing back the beginning of hunger pangs pulling at her.

She walked up to the counter and gave her basket to the cashier.

A shiver of awareness told her Tarian had come up beside her. He passed over his items and stood with his warm body brushing against her arm.

Melissa tried to wait as the cashier rang up their bill, but every pulse of his heartbeat, every brush of skin against skin, drove her to distraction.

"I'll wait outside," she said before striding out the door. Not like she had any money on her anyway.

Stepping into the night, she closed her eyes and tipped her head back. Humans had always feared the dark, but since her transformation it had become her haven. With her sensitive vampire vision, the dark road around her looked as brightly lit as if the sun were shining.

*Should have bought a pair of sunglasses,* she thought, remembering her designer collection at home with a wistful sigh.

Jogging down the steps, she glanced at the car before choosing to prowl toward the deserted alley between the convenience store and the building next to it. Stepping into the deeper shadows loosened some of the tension in her shoulders. She could do this. Their trip was about survival, and she'd always been particularly good at that game.

What had to stop was the longing that hit her every time she looked at her companion. He wasn't to be trusted, not given what he was, but her libido jumped into high gear when he so much as brushed against her.

*This reaction is ridiculous. You have more control than this.*

Even as she berated herself, a secret corner of her mind whispered that mates had an undeniable attraction that couldn't be tamed.

*Not my mate,* she thought. *The universe wouldn't be so cruel.*

"Melissa?"

She turned at the sound of her name to see Tarian striding forward. His gaze was firmly fixed on her, and not scanning for any threats that might await him in the gloom.

Her lips twitched at the thought. Anyone foolish enough to lie in wait for Tarian deserved the broken bones he'd dole out.

"Are you all right?" he asked.

She shook back her hair and nodded. "Fine. I just needed a minute."

Tarian stopped an arm's reach from her. His face was shadowed, but even with a bright light shining on him she wouldn't have been able to read his expression.

"You got everything?" she asked.

He lifted the white plastic bag dangling from his fingers.

"I'll pay you back when we reach the city."

He shrugged. "Buying you a hairbrush is the least I can do, given the circumstances."

He had a point.

"Okay, then we should get back on the road."

Tarian nodded, but neither of them moved.

Instead he took a step toward her.

"What are you doing?"

"Two more hours of uncomfortable silence sounds about as fun as taking a leisurely swim through shark infested waters."

"I'm not sure there's much we can do about it," she replied. "We are where we are."

He nodded. "You're right." His eyes flicked up to hers.

"Then again…"

The white bag dropped at their feet as he grabbed her by the waist and twirled her up against the store wall.

His lips captured hers, tasting, controlling.

Melissa pushed against his chest but he only wrapped his arms around her waist, pulling her closer. She nearly moaned at the sensation of his hard body rubbing against hers. Under different circumstances nothing would have stopped her from slipping her hands beneath his dark T-shirt and tracing the contours of his chest. Preferably with her tongue.

Tarian lifted her slightly, sliding one leg between hers so she balanced on his thigh. Desire pulsed through her as she fought the urge to rock against him.

His tongue traced the seam of her lips as he demanded entry, and her resolve weakened.

*Push him away,* her mind commanded. *Stand strong.*

She knew caution was the better part of valor. Right up to the moment she parted her lips.

Tarian took full advantage of her moment of weakness. He invaded her, consumed her, dominated her. There were a million reasons to push him away, but all her body craved was more.

His hands slid along her thighs, and she felt the heat of his touch even through the cheap denim. Need pulsed within her, just as it had the first time they'd touched.

Her fangs ached in her gums. The desire to bite, to taste Tarian, nearly overwhelmed her. Hunger mixed with lust in a powerful, intoxicating combination. She needed him. Needed him in a way she hadn't needed anyone before.

The tips of her fangs pushed free, and she couldn't stop

herself from scraping them oh so lightly against his tongue.

Tarian jerked under her hands as a tiny bead of blood welled into her mouth. There was no biting back the delicious moan that broke free from her throat. It was just the smallest taste, a minute burst of flavor, but the experience nearly brought her to her knees. Never in all her years had she tasted anything as addicting as him. Something was different about his blood. Something that called to her on the most basic of levels. The predator in her roared for more. She'd never get enough of him.

His hand slid down her spine to the curve of her waist, and she nearly purred at the caress. She craved more, wanted to feel his fingers trailing over her naked skin as she arched beneath him.

It was getting harder to think. There was a reason she shouldn't be doing this. Surely there was. But right now the only question on her mind was whether or not the shadows were dark enough to hide their activities if she were to shred their clothes and take him right there.

*Bad idea*, her inner voice whispered.

She didn't want to listen to logic or remember all the reasons why she shouldn't trust him. All she wanted was to prolong this perfect, maddening feeling.

With a groan, she pushed him back.

Tarian stared at her, lust clear in his gaze, with his hands still clenched around her waist.

"That was your grand idea to diffuse the tension?" she demanded.

His grin was almost boyish. "Couldn't hurt to try."

A smile tugged at her lips though she fought it back.

"At least now you'll believe me when I tell you I've

never touched you with any aim other than getting you into bed."

Her smile slipped from her lips as she looked up at him.

He arched a brow at her silence and caught her wrist. She didn't protest when he pressed her hand firmly against his hard erection.

"Think I'm faking that?" he demanded.

Unlikely. Her fingers curled around him instinctively, causing Tarian to hiss in pleasure.

"You could be a fantastic actor," she offered.

He arched a brow, silently questioning the ridiculousness of her statement.

Did she think he was acting? He might be. After all, there had to be more to the story than a necromancer desiring a vampire and deciding to date her. But if he hadn't helped his grandfather kidnap her, then what reason would he have for pretending to want her?

In a relationship wrought with lies, perhaps that one detail was true. Maybe he did want her just as much as she did him. A wave of relief surged through her, so strong it nearly sent her to her knees. She hadn't admitted, even to herself, how much she wanted this one thing to be true. Knowing she hadn't been the only one caught in the whirlwind of desire that claimed her every time they touched gave her strength. In this, at least, they were on even footing.

"Melissa," he said, giving her a little shake.

"All right," she yielded. "You want me."

Some of the tension eased from his body. "That's something at least."

"Doesn't change anything," she forced herself to say. He didn't need to know how much she'd wanted to hear their time together had mattered, even if only in a physical way.

"Nothing important," he agreed. His fingers found her chin and tipped her face up toward his. "But at least you know you've got the power to bring a necromancer to his knees."

"That silver tongue of yours will get you in trouble."

"Maybe you'll believe me one day." He pulled her close, his mouth a tantalizing breath away from hers.

"Sure, when the sun rises in the West. But I wouldn't hold my breath if I were you."

"Maddening woman."

"My middle name."

A smile tugged at his lips as he drew fingers down her cheek. "We need to get back on the road."

"Miles to go and all that." It would be so easy to close the distance. To press her lips to his and let him block out the world for another few moments. Her gaze flicked to his lips.

"Exactly."

*Step back,* she ordered herself. *You have more willpower than this.*

Unfortunately.

Melissa stepped out of his hold, mourning the loss of his touch even as she tried to convince herself she didn't. Her body didn't care what Tarian was. All it wanted was more of his pleasure-inspiring touches.

Grabbing the plastic bag from the ground, she headed for the car. With every step she felt Tarian at her back like a silent shadow. One she was far too attuned to.

Though to give credit where it was due, the silence in the car was far less uncomfortable when they pulled back onto the road. Instead of brooding over Tarian using her for his own purposes, her mind had his kiss on repeat. If only he could shake her distrust as easily as he stirred her libido, this trip might not be the nightmare she'd feared.

• • •

He'd made a mistake. He shouldn't have kissed her. Shouldn't have given in to temptation.

In the grand scheme of things, the feelings of two beings made no difference whatsoever. They had a mission to complete. One that did not necessitate any more contact than was needed to ensure their survival.

He'd had no reason to kiss her.

Except she'd looked at him with such loathing. Such distrust. It should be nothing new. After all, he'd destroyed his fair share of her species over the years. But he'd never held one first. Never seen the way they laughed, enjoyed the sound of their voice, hungered for their touch.

Not until Melissa.

With her, he couldn't separate what he knew had to be done and what he wanted to do for his selfish own ends. The opinions of her kind never mattered to him—except this time it was everything.

He didn't want her to hate him.

Tarian closed his eyes at the ridiculous thought. Their happy ending would be reaching New York and having Melissa warm up to him enough to stop the axe that was about to fall on his people. Nothing more. Her forgiveness was not part of the equation.

And then she'd looked at him, her expression so lost he'd reacted without thinking. All that mattered was wiping the desolation off her face.

Now he had to pay the price. The taste of her lingered on his lips. The memory of her fingers sliding through his hair, her body pressing intimately against his, ran on a constant loop in his mind. And, like a starving man, he craved more.

*Get a grip.* He could keep his hands to himself, and not give her yet another reason to dislike his race. This mission was too important to entangle with inconvenient feelings. More than just their lives depended on their success.

*I will be strong,* he promised. Strong enough to protect her from anything.

Even himself.

# Chapter Nine

Melissa couldn't remember ever being as happy to see a Motel 6 sign as she was right then. They'd spent the last half an hour looking for a place to stop for the night and though the silence had been far more companionable since their stop, a break from Tarian would be a welcome respite.

"Motel just ahead," she said.

Tarian turned to follow her pointing finger. "Just in time."

The dawn tugged at the edges of her senses, reminding her soon she'd have to seek shelter. The motel was as good a place as any. With a bit of luck, she'd be in her own room, away from the addicting necromancer in no time. She needed some distance before they got back on the road tomorrow. Tarian would be able to trap her with sweet words and tantalizing caresses if she wasn't careful, and she didn't want to stumble into any more mistakes where the man was concerned. Time apart would give her a chance to breathe and harden her resolve to keep her hands to herself.

As she drove into the parking lot she noted the large number of cars. "We might have to find something else," she said.

Tarian checked his watch. "Let's grab anything they have. We're pressing our luck if we keep looking."

"Next time you flee a pack of maniacs, stop to grab a cell with Google Maps."

"I'll make a note of that," he drawled.

*He probably doesn't want me around a phone,* she mused. Smart man. Though she wouldn't call for a rescue, she'd never promised not to contact her family to let them know she was safe. Surely there was no harm in that.

*Hotels have phones.* She just needed to wait until Tarian gave her an opening.

Tarian pulled the motel door open for her as they walked into reception. A sleepy night clerk jerked upright when they entered.

"Welcome to Motel 6," he said. "Checking in?"

"Do you have any rooms available for the day? I know the timing is awkward."

"When will you be checking out?" the receptionist said, glancing at the clock.

"Sunset," Melissa replied.

"I'll have to bill you for two nights." He shrugged in apology. "Or you can wait and check in at noon."

"Two nights is fine," Tarian replied. "Do you have a room?"

"Two rooms," Melissa put in.

The clerk checked his computer before nodding. "There's one standard king bed non-smoking available."

"Anything else?" Melissa asked. "Or at least something with separate beds?"

A few more clicks of the mouse were followed by a headshake. "All booked. That's our last room."

Of course it was. Melissa wondered if she could shake her fists at the universe without having her sanity questioned. Looked like her bad luck had struck again.

"The king is fine," Tarian said as he pulled out his wallet. "Paying by cash."

After only a few minutes, the receptionist handed over the key. "Second floor, on your right," he said.

Melissa followed Tarian into the elevator. Though it wasn't the outcome she'd counted on, at least they'd secured shelter from the sun.

That left only one other rising problem.

"This isn't too bad," Tarian said as he unlocked their room. "The curtains look thick. You should be safe for the day."

"Excellent news," she said, eying the phone on the bed stand.

The room was far more spacious than their last one. At least this motel boasted a cheap level of cleanliness and comfort. If worse came to worse, she could sleep in the small closet to escape the daylight.

"We can get back on the road as soon as you wake," he told her.

"Sounds like a plan. Want to use the shower first?"

His lips curved as he moved away from the window. "I can do that after you're out," he said. Reaching the side table, he grabbed the phone and disconnected the plug and phone jack. "Not that you were trying to get rid of me, I'm sure."

Melissa sighed. "Is that really necessary?"

He turned back to her, phone in hand. "Do you trust me?"

She stayed silent.

"Then it's necessary. Can't risk angering your vengeful father more than he already is."

He opened the door and disappeared into the hall.

She chewed on her lower lip, debating whether a phone call was worth fighting over. He didn't have her vampiric strength after all. If he didn't use his magic, she could overpower him.

But that was a dangerous "if" to bet on.

Tarian reappeared, his hands empty. For a moment he simply watched her, back against the closed door.

"Make any decisions?" he asked.

She turned away, not liking that he could read her thoughts so easily. "I don't want to fight again." Ignoring him, she crossed to the wide bed and collapsed backward onto it, bouncing twice on the springy mattress. The tight muscles in her body unwound, as if she'd been waiting for this moment the whole night trapped in the cramped car. It felt so good to simply stretch.

Closing her eyes, she tried to block out her partner and enjoy a few moments of respite.

The mattress dipped beside her, and she opened one eye to see Tarian, one arm bent to keep him upright while he lay by her side.

She'd been speaking the truth when she'd said she didn't want to fight. It took too much energy she didn't have. Instead, she allowed her eyelids to fall once more and avoided thinking about the man beside her.

Silence stretched, wrapping around them far more intimately than it had in the car. She supposed that's what happened when you added a bed into the equation.

She didn't want to open her eyes. Didn't want to acknowledge him. Just for a moment she wished she could push pause on the chaos she'd been dragged into. Three days ago she'd been doodling his name on her files, and now he was both her enemy and her rescuer. The ground was shifting beneath her feet, and she had no idea how to regain her balance.

There were a thousand questions she should put to him. Information she should seek about Dominic and the rebel necromancers. About their trip and what would happen when they reached safety. About him and the reason he'd dated her in the first place.

But it was a far different question that slipped passed her lips.

"Would you ever have told me what you are?"

He didn't reply immediately, and she didn't open her eyes. The question was revealing. It showed a vulnerability she'd rather have kept hidden. But exhaustion and the intimate silence were working against her.

"I don't know."

A curious pang twisted in her chest. His answer shouldn't hurt. He was a necromancer, after all. No matter what they'd started in the city, she could never be with him in the way she'd planned. It shouldn't matter that he'd never intended to be honest in their relationship.

"You wouldn't have given me the slightest chance had you known the truth."

"No," she agreed. She would have run from him as fast as her feet could carry her. "So why'd you do it?" She opened her eyes and turned her head toward him. "Was it just to see if you could get the better of a lonely vampire desperate for a little attention?"

He didn't so much as blink as she threw back the words he'd used at Dominic's dinner. Until she'd asked her question, she hadn't even realized how heavily the phrase had weighed on her. No matter what game he'd been playing when they'd first met, she didn't want him to see her as some desperate vampire he could use for his own amusement.

"I came after you to stop a war," he said instead, avoiding her question. "I would have come for any vampire in your position."

She didn't flinch. Points to her.

Tarian reached out to touch her cheek. "But my good intentions don't account for the panic I felt when I heard you were gone."

Melissa held still, waiting for him to continue.

"I lied about my species," he told her. "But never, not even for a moment, did I lie about wanting you. You're not just some lonely vampire I used to entertain myself."

A painful hope tugged at her even as she tried to battle it back with reason. "I'd be a fool to believe your words," she said.

"Doesn't make them less true."

Not for the first time, Melissa felt out of her depth. For years she'd watched her father play every political and strategic game known to man, but they hadn't prepared her for Tarian. How much of what he told her was a lie, and how much was truth? He'd promised not to use his magic on her so long as she stayed with him. Seducing her would be an easy way to bring her under his control. His attraction might be real, but that wouldn't stop him from using it to his advantage.

She had to be strong. To keep him at arms length. If she couldn't believe him, then she had to avoid letting her libido take charge. Tarian was one temptation that could be hazardous to her health. And heart.

"I need to go out," she said, pushing up from the bed and the clinging intimacy it inspired.

"What?" he asked as he sat up. "Dawn is coming up fast."

"I know. But a girl's gotta eat."

Understanding lit his eyes. "You're hungry."

"Gold star." She threaded her fingers through her hair. "I've only had one small glass of blood in two nights."

"We're not exactly in an urban center."

Melissa shrugged. "I have to find something. Surely there'll be early morning joggers or someone I can snack on. You have to love athletes. They're like drinking a diet." When he arched a skeptical brow she added, "Plus there's always the clerk downstairs if I get desperate."

"Or there's a far easier solution." He tugged off his jacket. "No."

Tarian arched a brow. "You're hungry. I'm offering."

Longing snaked through her before she battled it back. "I'm not feeding from you."

"Give me a good reason why not?"

Because feeding was intimate, and she couldn't handle more "intimate" with this man. The tiny taste she'd had in the alley still weighed heavily on her mind. All she had to do was glance at his neck, and she wanted to lick her lips in anticipation.

"Legend says drinking more than a drop or two of necromancer blood gives them power over us," she said instead.

A harsh laugh broke from him. "Look at your history books, Melissa. Your people did a damn fine job of drinking half my race dry. As we are the ones hiding in rural towns, I think you can safely assume there are no ill effects to drinking our blood. Now quit stalling. You're starving."

Her stomach rumbled as if to punctuate his words.

"I can hold out till tomorrow night," she said instead. "When I'll have more time to hunt."

"If you starve, you're too young to control the bloodlust it will inspire."

She narrowed her eyes. The damn man wasn't wrong, but no one liked having their weaknesses thrown in their face.

Melissa paced the length of the room. Going hunting this close to dawn was never a safe option. Nor was leaving bite marks on the clerk.

But she didn't trust herself with Tarian, even if the thought of sinking her fangs into him did fill her with a surge of possessive delight.

*Just think of him as any random stranger in your past*, she ordered herself. *A meal is a meal. Don't make it into more than food. A few gulps and that's it. Home free.*

"Come here, Melissa."

She turned to see him holding out a hand to her. Still she hesitated. She wanted to hate him. Wanted to rail at him for making her feel small and foolish. And instead her mouth watered, and her body yearned to go to him.

"I'm running out of ways to say no."

"Think about this logically. This is the safest choice."

"I've never been a room service kind of girl. I'd rather go out for a bite."

He shook his head. "Don't be ridiculous. You know I'm right."

She fought back the urge to hiss at him. "Indeed. I suppose I should be grateful you're not making me beg at your feet for a meal, necromancer."

His expression blanked.

Hot shame tore through her even as she tried to tell herself it didn't matter that she'd tossed his generous offer back in his face. She shouldn't care about a necromancer's feelings. Shouldn't be caught in this confusing situation in the first place. But logic didn't erase the fact that she did care about the disappointment she read in his eyes.

"Dammit," she said, whirling to turn her back to him. "This isn't fair."

She hated to show weakness in front of an enemy, and yet her body was betraying her. Dawn pulled at her senses, reminding her of the ever-ticking clock that was her reality. If she was going to feed, it had to be soon.

Gentle hands smoothed over her shoulders, and she stiffened. She hadn't even heard him move she was so agitated.

"I know," he whispered against her ear, his voice low. "There is very little about this situation I can make right. But this, Melissa, is something I can give you."

"Doesn't this unnerve you?" she asked. "We have our fears of necromancers but you have some of us as well. Our fangs are our greatest weapon."

His thumb brushed over her nape. "I trust you not to drain me."

*Brave or naive?* she wondered, turning in his arms. She could take him out. Leave his corpse in the closet and take her chances on her own. But even as the thought crossed her mind, she knew she couldn't do it.

*Because I need him to stop Lucian from raining havoc down on us all,* she told herself. Not because she'd miss him.

A wry smile twisted his lips. "Think of it this way. In another life, we probably would have ended up here eventually."

She knew what he meant. If Dominic hadn't interfered, they'd be happily dating in New York instead of trekking across the country. She'd be gossiping with Abbey about her excellent match and counting down the hours until she could see him again.

She'd be thinking she'd finally found her mate.

Sorrow shook her as she mourned that shattered life, which would never exist again. The necromancers had done more than kidnap her. They'd also robbed her of a relationship she'd waited decades to find.

"You would have let me bite you?" she asked. "Even without me knowing what you were?"

"Our blood doesn't taste different from any other run-of-the-mill immortal," he replied. "There would be no danger in it."

"I wasn't talking about exposing you." His kind did not sign up for vampire feedings. Nor did they give away valuable advantages as he had with the rield. And they never risked their own safety to help an enemy.

Tarian wasn't just challenging her preconceptions of his kind. He was smashing them into a million pieces.

"It's all right," he said, reassuring her, when it should have been the other way around. "Take what you need."

*He needs you healthy. This helps his cause as much as it does yours,* she reasoned. Except, right then the outside world felt very far away.

Taking his wrist, she turned it up toward her mouth.

"No," he said when she started to lean down. "Not there."

His hands slid around her waist to pull her closer as he tipped his head back.

She wanted to protest the intimate touch, but it caused her too much joy to demand he stop. Instead she stepped closer, her gaze locking on the pounding pulse in his throat.

Closing her eyes, she breathed in his unique scent of musk and magic. Her mouth watered as she pressed her lips to his neck. Life beat so close to the surface of his skin. Parting her lips, she dragged her tongue over his pulse.

Tarian groaned. His fingers tightened around her waist.

Her fangs lengthened, and she scraped them gently against his skin.

"Do it," he whispered against her ear.

She bit down without any further urging.

Melissa moaned in pleasure as his blood touched her tongue. Had she ever tasted anything as good as him? She drew a deep sip, savoring the richness.

Tarian's hand fisted in her hair as she drank. A vampire's bite could be pleasurable for their victims if they wanted it to be, and Melissa couldn't help herself from sharing the joy she felt with him.

Every sip she took tasted like pure energy. She felt her body grow stronger and repair the damage the sun had caused. But more than heal, Tarian's blood excited her, thrilled her.

He waltzed her backward until their legs bumped against the bed. They tumbled onto the soft mattress without Melissa ever giving up her prize.

Without conscious thought, she kicked a leg astride him as she drank. His taste was intoxicating. The desire she felt being around him amplified a thousand fold with his blood on her tongue.

Melissa rocked against him as she moved in time to her swallows. Lust laced through her veins, enthralling her as much as the blood did. The urge to laugh, to touch, to pleasure pounded through her. Given the rock-hard erection between her thighs, it was a craving Tarian shared.

Melissa wanted to drink forever. All too soon she reached the point where his heart shuddered as it tried to pump less blood through his body.

The predator in her demanded she finish what she'd started. She could take it all, every last drop.

But then there'd be no more. No more blood. No more Tarian.

And she had a horrifying suspicion she needed them both.

With a last long pull, she reared back.

"My God," Tarian breathed, his eyes glazed with pleasure.

Melissa drew her tongue over the small puncture wounds to clean them of every last drop. Pressing her hands against his chest, she pushed herself up even though all she wanted to do was snuggle closer.

"I never knew," he said. Tarian reached up to run his thumb over her mouth. She saw a smear of red across his skin when he removed his hand and instinctively caught it in her mouth.

Her tongue swirled over the pad of his thumb as she swallowed the last taste of him.

"Good?" he asked.

"Delicious," she replied. She fought back the desire to roll her hips against his straining erection. Vampires could get blood drunk when they found a truly excellent victim, and she feared Tarian might just be her drug of choice.

"Your eyes are red."

Melissa blinked, knowing what it meant. When a vampire's true nature pushed to the surface their eyes reflected that loosening of control. Her eyes hadn't changed color during a feed since she'd been a young fledgling. Rarely did they darken even during a night of great sex.

Yet Tarian shattered that tight rein she used to hold herself in check.

"I like it," Tarian said as he hooked a hand around her nape.

She should resist, but when he tugged her down, common sense deserted her. His blood pumped through her veins, creating a connection she'd never experienced before. All she wanted was one more touch.

His lips met hers and ignited the desire she was trying to keep banked.

Melissa writhed over top of him. Her hands tugged at his T-shirt in an attempt to work it over his head.

His mouth left hers for the briefest second as he pulled the material over his head. Melissa nearly purred with pleasure when she looked down at his sculpted body. His golden skin offered stark contrast to her pale fingers. They were different in every way.

But that didn't stop her from pressing her mouth to his

chest and licking his essence off his skin.

"Yes," Tarian hissed when her tongue lapped over a nipple. One hand tangled in her hair while the other fisted in the sheets. He was trying to be good, and she appreciated the gesture. It gave her free reign to play with him as she'd dreamed about.

Her fingers glided across his body, and she felt the muscles in his abdomen tighten at her touch.

Instinct urged her to remember he was a necromancer, not a lover, but the longer she spent in his company the further the line blurred. Right then she wasn't undulating against an enemy. He was simply Tarian. A man she wanted to be hers.

Melissa traced one light fingertip along the waistband of his jeans, pausing just under his navel.

She rolled her eyes up to his as she began to kiss her way down his chest. Tarian bucked beneath her, urging her on with his body, if not his words.

Her fingers reached for the fly of his jeans, just as the world spun before her eyes.

Desire drained away as it became an effort to keep her head up.

"Tarian," she breathed, resting her forehead against his chest.

"Melissa?" He reached down for her and rolled her onto the bed. "What are you—?" He paused and glanced at the electric clock on the nightstand. "Bloody hell," he said. "Sweetheart, it's dawn."

"You've got to be kidding me," she groaned.

The intoxication of his blood was fading, leaving behind only the sting of embarrassment. Not only had she been craving a man she should be holding at arms length, she'd gone and riled him up with promises she'd never be able to follow through on. Melissa hadn't miscalculated her timing so badly in decades.

His chuckles grated her already frazzled nerves. "This isn't funny," she said, but it was hard to be severe when she could barely keep her eyes open.

"I'm laughing at myself," he assured her. "Can you crawl under the covers?"

She rolled onto her stomach and tried to shimmy toward the head of the bed with varying degrees of success. Flopping around like a fish on dry land in front of the man she'd just been pawing did not help alleviate any of her humiliation.

"I'll take that as a no," he said, a trace of humor in his voice.

Tarian swept her up into his arms. "Let yourself sleep, Melissa," he said, pressing a kiss to her forehead.

"Embarrassed," she breathed as he laid her head on the pillow.

"I told you before. Anticipation is a good thing."

She felt his fingers caress her cheek but couldn't find the strength to open her eyes as she fell into unconsciousness.

• • •

Tarian collapsed into the chair he'd pulled up next to the bed. She was out like a light. If he were a gentleman, he'd cover her with a blanket and hit the shower. Instead, he couldn't drum up the will to move.

Her lashes cast dark semicircles onto her creamy skin. A lock of hair fell across her cheek, and he couldn't stop himself from reaching out to brush it back into place.

He traced his fingertips along her jaw before sitting back. Melissa was always beautiful, but he'd never seen her this way before. There was no fear, no confusion on her face. She looked utterly peaceful.

And terribly vulnerable.

The past flashed through his mind, when he had hunted during the day, seeking vampires just as vulnerable as the one before him. No hesitation had ever gripped him in those dark days during the wars. He'd never doubted he was destroying evil.

Yet the woman before him was anything but.

"I made my peace with your kind," he whispered to her. That acceptance didn't account for the feelings rising within him each time he touched her, however. Hell, his vow to keep his hands to himself had lasted less than two hours. How was he supposed to survive the next few days?

"What are you doing to me?"

There was no answer to be found. A vampire was tying him in knots, and when her lips were on his, he didn't seem to mind one damn bit.

Pushing from the chair, he reached out and flicked the blanket over Melissa for extra protection from any stray sunbeams. He paced into the bathroom, running a hand over his face. Shower first, and then he'd deal with planning their route for the next day. One thing was for sure. After his last bout with Melissa, sleep would be a long time coming.

"Shower," he said to his reflection. "And let's make it a cold one."

# Chapter Ten

The endless driving was not quite as fun the second night as it had been the first.

Melissa sat in the passenger seat and watched the flat landscape fly by outside her window. They'd passed a WELCOME TO OKLAHOMA sign a few hours back, so at least they were on the right path.

"We need to stop soon," Tarian said. "You might have fed last night but I'm going to need a real meal to refuel. There are only so many power bars one can eat."

The reminder of her last meal brought a blush to her cheeks. When she'd opened her eyes after her day's sleep, the memory of her ill-fated make out session had been burned in her mind. She'd actually dreaded pulling off the cover that had kept her safe from the sun.

But when she had, Tarian had greeted her with a smile and the suggestion that they get on the road as quickly as possible.

She turned to glance at her companion. Other men might have been put out that she'd started something she couldn't finish, but not Tarian. Did nothing rattle the man?

"There are lights up ahead," she said, instead of the prying questions she wanted to ask. "Maybe there'll be somewhere to stop."

"I'd kill for a burger." He shot her a wide grin. "Gotta keep my iron up."

Which meant he wasn't opposed to feeding her again. A wave of relief washed over her. Not that she couldn't survive a few days of hunger until they reached home. Still, some part of her relaxed to hear he didn't regret an act that was as vital to her as breathing was to him.

The small town grew on the horizon, and she hoped there'd be somewhere to stop. It might lengthen their travel time, but keeping her partner healthy helped both of them in the long run.

"Ye old timey diner," he pointed out, maneuvering the car into the small parking lot. "Looks decent enough for a quick bite."

"Fine by me," she agreed.

The truck stop looked like it'd been modeled after a fifties diner. Or perhaps it simply hadn't been updated in decades. Either way, they found a spot to sit in one red vinyl booth. A ragged looking waitress came up to them immediately with two menus and two waters.

"You two are out late," she commented.

"Road trip," Tarian replied. "I'll take as big a cup of coffee as you can muster up and an equally large burger. Rare."

"Coming right up." She turned to Melissa. "And for

you?"

"Not hungry," she replied, holding out her menu.

"Need some meat on those bones, sugar," the waitress said as she took the menus and walked away.

Melissa sighed. The woman wasn't wrong. She'd grown up in a time that had valued more voluptuous figures and had always thought it was a far healthier alternative to the current model craze. Her vampirism, however, kept her from ever achieving the more womanly figure she admired.

"I think you're perfect," Tarian commented as he sipped his water.

The words brought a smile to her face even as they sent a shiver down her spine. "You're biased, since you're trying to keep me in a good mood so I don't desert you."

"Believe what you wish." He leaned back against the booth with a tired sigh.

"I'll drive the next leg," she offered. "It'll be hours before exhaustion catches up with me."

"Deal."

The waitress hustled back with his coffee, and Tarian groaned in pleasure when he tasted the hot beverage.

"Life got a whole lot easier after this drink was invented," he said, inhaling the aroma with closed eyes.

Melissa blinked. He was older than coffee? Racking her brain, she tried to remember when coffee had come into vogue. Certainly by her time it was a standard in many homes.

When she'd met Tarian in Fated Match's reception room she'd assumed they were of similar age. A careless mistake on her part. An immortal's appearance didn't necessarily correlate to their chronological years. Strength, however, grew with the passage of time. If he was old, then he'd be a strong opponent against any foe. Perhaps even her father.

"I can hear you worrying," he said, not bothering to open his eyes.

Melissa was used to hearing the heartbeat of those around her and noting when it raced with excitement or shuddered in fear. That someone else could read her body's changes in the same way unnerved her.

"Looking forward to getting home," she replied.

"Nope. Not it." His blue eyes flickered open. "What's going on in that head of yours?"

She debated asking her questions. They had a decent enough truce going. More than decently, really, considering the activities of last night. Prying into his past could change that.

Or worse, it could cause her to become even more infatuated with the damn necromancer than she already was.

"I was wondering about you," she answered, meeting his gaze.

Tarian tilted his head. "I told you, there isn't much to tell."

"Such lies," she murmured.

He set his cup down before giving her his full attention. "If you want to delve into my past, Melissa, I'll be demanding quid pro quo."

Her mother's face flashed across her mind. Tarian might be on her side right now but who knew what the future held? Giving him more ammunition against her could be a mistake.

*Curiosity killed the cat,* she thought. Then again, maybe the cat had died happy.

"Where were you before America?" she asked.

"Europe."

"And when exactly did coffee come to Europe?"

A tiny smile twisted his lips. "My history is a little rusty, but I believe a pope in the 1600's is to thank for its rise in popularity."

Her nails gouged into the vinyl beneath her. That definitely beat her single century.

"Were you young when coffee changed the mornings of Europeans across the continent?"

He held her gaze. "No."

Melissa licked her lips as she contemplated her next question. "Did you fight in the necromancer wars?"

This time he wasn't so forthcoming. His fingers tapped against the laminate tabletop. "Are you sure you want to know, Melissa?"

She swallowed. If he had, then he was old. Not a few hundred years, give or take, but really, really old. According to her history books, the wars had raged across Eastern Europe in the early fourteenth century. If he'd been a part of them, that not only meant he was a strong warrior, but he was qualified to be an elder, if necromancers had one.

"I want to know," she said.

Tarian inclined his head. "I was only a few decades old when I fought in the wars with my father."

She exhaled out of habit. "Well, hell. I always did have a thing for older men."

The waitress arrived with Tarian's burger, and Melissa welcomed the respite. Her father had battled the necromancers. The idea that the two men currently most important in her life could have met years before she was even born made her head hurt.

"You must have hated us," she said.

Tarian's eyes flicked to her before he turned his attention back to his meal. "Yes," he agreed. "For many years."

*And now?* But she couldn't voice the question fearing what the answer would be.

"Before I came into your life, had you ever met a necromancer?"

She ran her nail along the chrome lining of the table as she contemplated owing him her own answers about the past. "No," she breathed.

Lucian had been very careful to keep her protected when she was younger, and by the time she'd grown, the modern world had exploded. Necromancers had been pushed further and further back into the less populated areas of the country.

"But you feared us."

"Given the history it's only natural that—"

"Yes or no, Melissa."

"Yes," she said, lifting her eyes to his.

"Because you were taught we were evil, without ever having the chance to form your own opinion. Can you imagine what it's like growing up as a necromancer child?" He took a bite of his burger.

"You can't blame us for fearing creatures who can command us like puppet masters."

"Perhaps not," he replied. "But I can blame you for turning the rest of the supernatural world against us. Our powers only work on the death races, and yet even living, flesh and blood immortals fear us. Against a werewolf I'd be almost as useless as a human." Tarian pointed a french fry at her. "The fact of the matter is, vampires rule our world, and your prejudice became everyone's prejudice. We never had a chance."

"The necromancers haven't exactly been a peaceful race," she said. "That I'm sitting in this diner is proof of that."

"Where did being peaceful ever get us?" he asked. "Whether we behaved or not, we were condemned."

Melissa turned away from him, not liking the uncomfortable doubt worming its way into her mind. She remembered the child at Dominic's ranch and the sad resignation in her eyes. Had the vampires been too zealous in their effort to protect themselves?

"Preaching world peace, are you?" she asked.

A sardonic smile twisted his lips. "We've spent days together without any mortal injury. Surely that proves our two kinds can coexist."

"You're quite the idealist to have been caught up fighting wars."

A bleak hopelessness shuttered his eyes. "It took me many centuries to come to my beliefs," he said. "When the wars were fought, I thought the only way we could survive was to eradicate your people."

A beat of silence passed as she pondered his words. Giving in to the urge to ask her most pressing question, Melissa leaned forward, crossing her arms on the table. "Why did you pursue me?"

Tarian blinked. "What?"

"You wouldn't tell me before. Tell me now."

No expression passed over his face as he regarded her in silence.

"I bullied Abbey into setting up our date, but for it to

work, you had to agree," she continued. "You knew who I was. Hell, even if you hadn't recognized me, you're as old as the hills. You'd have been able to sense me the second you walked through the doors. So why did we ever end up at Celeste's?"

He polished off the last of his burger as she wondered whether he'd yield this time. When they'd first started this trip he'd been right—she wouldn't have believed a word he said. But now... She didn't know when things had changed, but they had. Whatever answer he gave, good or bad, she'd believe it.

"I knew there'd be complications," he said.

"But you did it anyway."

"Yes."

"Why?"

Pushing his plate away, he met her steady gaze. "Because I was serious when I said I wanted to find my mate, and I have never, not once in nearly seven hundred years, reacted to a woman the way I did to you."

Her jaw dropped. Her heart clenched. He hadn't meant his words the way they'd sounded. Couldn't possibly.

But hadn't she felt the exact same way when they'd first locked eyes across the pink-and-white waiting room?

"There has never been a vampire-necromancer pairing," she whispered.

"Because it isn't possible, or because there was never an opportunity?" he asked. "We could check the Fated Match website right now, and I guarantee the number of necromancers signed up would be less than a handful. Hard to mingle when every other race runs at the mere sight of you."

"What are you saying, Tarian? We were meant to be?"

The pause before he responded was the longest moment of her hundred years. Part of her hoped he scoffed at the notion just as she had. A deeper, more secret part, however, waited for a different outcome.

"No," he said at last. "My mate will never abhor me. I was attracted to you, still am, but you're not the woman I've waited lifetimes to find."

*I'm not bleeding,* she told herself. *His words don't affect me.* But his denial that she could ever be more to him than a bedmate cut her in ways she hadn't thought possible. She'd rather face a brush with the sun than the absolute certainty in his eyes.

*My luck strikes again. Perfect man, imperfect circumstances.*

"Good," she said, lifting her chin so he'd never know how his confession pained her. "I feel exactly the same. Obviously our flirtation in New York was ill conceived."

"It seems we agree on something at last." He waved at the waitress to bring the bill.

Melissa gazed out the dark window by her side. It didn't matter what he said or what he believed. All that mattered was getting home. That was her end goal. Not roping Tarian into her life along the way. It was good that they'd dispelled any lingering doubts she'd had. It wasn't like she'd been hoping for some star-crossed happily ever after with the man. Had she?

"Thank you," she said, not looking at him.

Tarian turned to her, passing cash to the waitress as he did. "What?"

"I know you came for me in order to help your people, not mine. You might even have come because you thought I was…important to you. It doesn't matter. Whatever your reasons, thank you. For saving me."

He sat in silence for a long moment before replying. "I have many regrets in my life."

Melissa closed her eyes as she waited for his next words. Surely he'd add helping her to the list. The ungrateful vampire heiress who couldn't look past her own prejudice, even when her life depended on it.

"Rescuing you is not one of them."

She turned to him then. There was nothing pleasant in his expression. No joy, no hint of hope. He knew as well as she did that no matter what became of their romance on this road trip, it wouldn't last past the city limits.

*A relationship with an expiration date,* she thought. *No matter what choices you make on the road, they won't follow you home. Two more nights and you'll be safe in your own bed. Won't you regret not knowing what it felt like to be Tarian's, even if only for a night?*

"Here's your change, sugar," the waitress interrupted, setting the receipt back onto the table.

"Thank you," Tarian said, breaking eye contact with Melissa.

She mentally shook her head. When she pushed from the red booth she was back to her normal self. No regrets, no wishing things were different. A necromancer and a vampire had no future in today's modern world. Even if a part of her wished otherwise.

"After you," Tarian said, holding the door open for her.

"Thanks." She stepped out into the night and wished it held its usual comfort. Instead she wrapped her arms around herself and headed for the car.

They nearly reached it when a child's scream cut through

the night followed by the smell of burning rubber and the squeal of tires skidding against the asphalt.

"Tarian," she said, but he was already gone, running across the parking lot.

Melissa hesitated. She was alone. For the first time in days, no one watched her. She could use her speed to run as fast and as far as she could and never look back. Tarian might not be able to track her. She'd be free.

But that child's cry sliced through her mind. What if she could help?

*A human life,* her inner voice whispered. *What is that compared to yours?*

Melissa turned to look out over the flat plains around her. It'd be so easy, so simple. This was her chance to escape. She could leave behind the necromancer that challenged her beliefs and made her life far more complicated than it should have been. This was her chance to run and escape, not only her pursuers but also the looming choices she was going to have to make about Tarian. If she left now, she'd never have to fight her attraction for him again. She'd never have to contemplate the ramifications of yielding to that pulsing, ever present desire.

Instead her feet turned in the direction Tarian had run.

*Fool*, she thought even as she raced to the road. What she saw when she arrived, however, stopped her cold.

The human child was unharmed. She sat at Tarian's side with tears streaming down her face. In Tarian's hands lay a small furry shape.

Melissa sighed as she realized it was only a dead cat. It had probably caught the wrong end of a car and ended up splattered over the dusty road.

"No," the child moaned, reaching out to stroke her pet. "No, no, no."

Melissa walked closer as the urgency drained from her body. She was about to call out Tarian's name when he raised his hand.

Magic played over her skin. It brushed against her with a gentle touch that sent a shiver up her spine. Though her instinct was to fight it off, the power swirled around her without posing any threat.

Tarian dragged his finger through the cat's fur and before her eyes, the dead animal inhaled.

Both she and the child jumped in amazement.

"Take her straight to the vet," Tarian ordered in a low voice. "She has a lot of internal damage. Do you understand me?"

The little girl nodded solemnly.

"All right." He picked up the mewing cat and placed her in the child's arms. "Run," he said. "She doesn't have much time."

"Thanks," the human lisped before jetting off along the dark street.

Tarian watched the child go before turning his head in her direction.

At his dark expression Melissa took a step back despite herself. His magic still curled through the air, reaching out to her as if waiting for permission to pounce. Though she was unused to being cast in the role of prey and not predator, Melissa held completely still as she waited for him to get a handle on his magic. She hadn't been making idle threats the first night they'd been together. If he used his powers against her, she would fight tooth and nail to escape him.

The spell snapped when Tarian dragged a hand down his face. Magic recoiled from her, flooding back to its source.

"Sorry." His voice was rough. "Power high."

After her intoxication the night before she could relate to the drawbacks of using one's abilities. Still, she waited as he got to his feet and started toward her.

"I thought you would have run," he said when he got close enough.

"And you would have to spend the night tracking me down."

"Something like that."

She gazed past his shoulder at the small figure running in the distance. "I wanted to help."

"She wasn't hurt."

"Not physically."

He nodded. "The animal's spirit was clinging to life. It didn't want to leave its mortal." Tarian shrugged. "It cost me nothing to buy it more time."

"You couldn't heal it?"

He shook his head, reaching her at last. "My power is over the dead, not the living. I tied the spirit to the body for a brief window, but without human intervention the animal will die. If the vet is good, the damage will be repaired before my magic wears off. The cat will live, and hopefully, the child will think twice about running across a road."

"You just saved a life, even if only a small one. This isn't something to shrug away."

A wry smile twisted his lips. "You see me as death," he whispered. "But the act I just committed is one I've repeated a thousand times before. My powers can work both ways, Melissa. For good or for evil, just like any other person's abilities."

He walked away from her, back toward the car.

She should follow him, but she couldn't shake the miraculous scene she'd just witnessed. A being who should be dead was alive because of Tarian's intervention. An intervention he didn't see as anything out of the ordinary.

*We see them only as threats,* she realized. But their powers opened the possibility of so much more. Tonight a necromancer had offered joy and comfort, not death and destruction.

After seven hundred years, Tarian still didn't see his mercy as anything worthy of a second glance.

But she did.

Trailing after him, she studied his shadowed figure. Her life would be so much easier if Tarian would stop showing her unexpected facets of himself that she'd never hoped to find.

And stop filling her mind with thoughts no vampire should harbor about her enemy.

• • •

This hotel was by far the nicest they'd stayed in. Flicking on the lights, Melissa took in the double beds and white sheets. Everything was clean and crisp, definitely an improvement over the last couple places they'd stayed.

"I'm taking a shower," Tarian said.

She arched a brow. "Not worried I'll run?"

"Not anymore," he replied, closing the bathroom door behind him.

Melissa let herself fall backward onto the closest bed.

The last few hours of their drive had been silent. Not that she'd minded. Unlike the first night, it was not an uncomfortable quiet. Besides, she'd appreciated the extra time to sort through the revelations swimming in her mind.

She'd never really thought about the kind of life necromancers were forced to live. Never even imagined that they'd have a reason to protest their treatment. It shamed her that she'd held balls and fundraisers for every human rights charity in New York, and not once had she thought about the prejudices and disparities in her own community.

The sound of running water filled the air as she contemplated her next move. Tarian was keeping her close in order to help his cause when they reached the city, but maybe she could be more than merely a witness that not all necromancers were evil.

Crawling across the bed she reached for the phone on the nightstand. This time Tarian had been too preoccupied to strip their room of anything technological. With her companion occupied, this could be her only chance to contact her family. She wasn't going to waste it.

Luckily she'd never gotten used to the modern cell phone world with programmed numbers instead of good old-fashioned address books. The numbers of those most important to her were branded in her mind.

Her fingers paused over the keys as she debated who to call. Lucian would be impossible to calm over the phone but luckily for her, he now came attached at the hip to a far more serene mate.

The line rang as she waited for Abbey to pick up. Leaving a voicemail would be less than ideal.

"Hello?" Abbey said as the call connected. She sounded

tired, and Melissa winced at the time.

"Abbey," she said. "Hi."

The sounds of scrambling movements and rustling covers met her ears.

"Melissa?" Abbey demanded, her voice high-pitched. "Where are you? Are you all right? We'll come get you."

"No, listen. I'm fine. I'm on my way home right now. We should be there in two nights or so."

There was a pause. "We?"

"That's the other reason I'm calling," she said. "When I get to town I need to introduce Lucian to someone, and I need you to prep him on the idea so father doesn't rip him limb from limb."

"Does this have anything to do with Tarian's mysterious disappearance?"

"I don't know what you mean," she lied. The last thing she wanted was for Lucian to hunt down Tarian's home and discover his sister living within the city limits. "But I need you to start promoting the idea that not all necromancers are evil."

Abbey snorted. "I have an infinitely slim chance of accomplishing that."

"I've seen the way Lucian looks at you," she replied. "You can convince him of anything."

"Why should I? You can't tell me they aren't behind the kidnapping."

"Look, the people who took me don't stand for the whole group. Someone else is helping me and it's…challenging a lot of my previous beliefs."

"That's all well and good of you to have an open mind, but you have no idea the hell Lucian and I have gone through since you left."

"I'm sorry," she said. "I would never have put you in that situation if I had a choice."

"Be prepared for a whole army of bodyguards when you're home," Abbey said.

"Fine, but one problem at a time. Will you make sure Lucian is home two nights from now? We'll probably be in early, so I doubt he'll need to take the whole night off."

"If you think he's not going to yell at you and threaten to destroy the necromancers for ten hours straight, you really don't have much concept of what's been going on here."

She groaned. "Fair enough. I'll come up to the apartment as soon as we hit the city."

"With your friend."

"My rescuer," she stressed. "Father is not allowed to remove his head the second he steps through the door."

"I make no promises," Abbey said, her voice growing serious. "This situation is not okay, Melissa, and I'm not going to try and convince Lucian it is."

"I get that. Tell father I love him. I'll be home soon."

"Stay safe."

Melissa hung up the phone as she battled a pang of homesickness. How she wished she could just take a plane and not have to worry about showing up on Dominic's radar again.

"Finished?"

She turned to see Tarian stepping from the bathroom. Not only was he still fully clothed, his hair wasn't the least bit damp.

"You were testing me," she sighed. "Seriously?"

"I wanted a sense of how this would play out when we

reached the city, yes."

"Hope you got what you wanted."

"Somewhat." He glanced at his watch. "Get under the covers, Melissa. We cut it too close today."

Dawn already called to her, reminding her of her limitations. She kicked off her shoes and slid into her bed. Tarian walked over to draw the curtains and ensure she was protected from the sun.

"What happens when we reach New York?" she asked.

He sat on the edge of her bed, placing a hand on either side of her body as he leaned closer. "What do you mean?"

"Say this plays out exactly the way you are hoping. Do we shake hands and go our separate ways?"

His blue eyes flashed in the dim light. "What's the alternative?"

"I don't know."

He studied her for a long moment in silence. "Would you regret never seeing me again, Melissa?"

It was her turn to think. There was no denying the complications of a necromancer lover, but the man she'd learned about tonight was one she'd lament losing.

"Yes." The word hung in the air between them. One that opened possibilities they'd both been trying their best to ignore.

There was no joy in his eyes at her confession, and she understood why. It didn't really matter what they wanted in the grand scheme of things. Not when the safety of their people had to come first.

Reaching out a finger, he traced the curve of her cheek. "Walking away from you will be the hardest thing I've done in centuries."

The edges of the curtain glowed with the rise of the sun, and Melissa fought to keep her eyes open, wanting to see more of the tenderness she read on his face. Had anyone ever looked at her with such longing? She couldn't remember. Couldn't think of any man she'd been with before Tarian. He eclipsed all challengers without even trying.

"Sleep," he said, pulling up the cover. "We'll talk more tomorrow."

Tomorrow. Her last full night with him. Whatever decisions they might make about their fate, tomorrow was the time to make them.

Her eyes slipped closed as Tarian settled the covers over her head. One more night with her maddening man.

Perhaps the last one they'd ever share together.

# Chapter Eleven

Every instinct in his body screamed at once. Tarian shot awake, scanning the room for threats. Nothing so far, but it wouldn't stay that way.

He launched himself out of the bed as he checked his watch. Sunset would come soon, but not soon enough. Melissa was still dead to the world.

For a moment he debated waiting the few minutes it would take her to wake but knew they didn't have that kind of time. Grabbing the covers, he ripped them off the bed and looked down at his companion.

She looked peaceful in sleep. Completely unaware that their enemies were creeping closer with every passing second.

"Forgive me," he said as he pulled her up and slung her over his shoulder, fireman style. Abandoning the bag with their changes of clothes and toiletries, Tarian opened the door and glanced down the hallway. Empty. For now.

Some might accuse him of being paranoid, but he felt

the familiar itch in his mind of a necromancer moving closer. He didn't know how the hell Dominic had managed to track them, but he wasn't waiting around to find out.

Pulling the door closed behind him, he jogged down the hall. Elevators were out. There was no telling who'd be waiting when the doors opened.

He paused to check one of the fire evacuation plaques stapled into the wall and located the nearest stairwell.

Melissa shifted on his shoulder, life infusing slowly into her body.

"Hold on, sweetheart," he murmured as he set off for the stairs.

He rounded the corner just as his powers flared. Whoever was after them, they'd stepped onto their floor.

Tarian crashed into the stairwell and started running down the stairs. Just their luck that they'd stayed on the very top floor.

"Tarian?" He heard a sleepy voice say.

"I'm here," he replied, smoothing a hand over the back of her legs as he jogged to the next landing.

"What the— Tarian Drake set me down this instant!"

He heard the indignation and smiled. "Just a sec." Gripping her tightly, he allowed her to slip down his body and back to the ground.

Melissa blinked up at him, her eyes cloudy with sleep. "Want to tell me why I was over your shoulder and not in a nice soft bed?"

"Dominic found us," Tarian replied. He looked up the twisting stairs to make sure no one had come after them. "I don't know how he did it, but just before sunset I felt the presence of necromancers moving closer."

"You can GPS your own people?"

"Yes." He caught her hand and pulled her down the stairs.

"Seriously? Can all you guys do that?"

"No," he replied. "I have skills others of my kind do not."

"Because you're a ridiculously old man?"

He shot her a glare. "With age comes power." They took the stairs two at a time.

"Okay, so tell me you've got a master plan," Melissa asked, not even panting as she ran to keep up with his pace.

"'Don't get seen' is pretty much the extent of it so far."

"Elegant," she mocked. "But it beats the alternative. You realize if they use their necromancer mojo on me I won't be immune."

"Trust me, your liability had occurred to me." If only he'd managed to get the damn rield away from Dominic back at the ranch. It didn't escape him that he was fighting to protect a woman who would come at him with fangs and claws if any of his kin commanded her to.

"Anything in your bag of tricks to stop me from being influenced?" she asked as they rounded another corner.

"I already told you I can't make another rield on short notice."

"Then don't let me walk back into Dominic's clutches, okay?"

He wasn't immune to the thin thread of doubt in her voice. Pausing, he twirled her into his arms and forced her face up to his. "Dominic is never getting near you again," he vowed.

A soft smile lit her face. "Good to know," she replied before baring her fangs. "Not that I'm without my own talents."

"Try not to kill anyone," he said. "I probably have a distant cousin or two in the crowd."

Melissa pouted. "How about I promise not to not try to kill the bastards who kidnapped me?"

"Melissa," he warned.

"Fine," she capitulated with a sigh. "No mortal wounds if I can help it."

"Thank you." He kissed her quickly before twining his fingers through hers and pulling her once again down the stairs.

They practically flew down the flights as they raced for the ground. Finally the door to the lobby appeared before them.

Tarian gestured for her to stay back as he inched toward the door. She pressed her body against the wall as she waited to see if the exit was guarded.

With a last glance to ensure she was out of the way, Tarian eased the door open an inch.

The lobby came into view, as did the angry glare of the necromancer guarding the door.

He jumped back as the guard kicked the door open and burst into the stairwell.

*Protect Melissa,* he thought, his powers already flooding through his body. Tarian stepped forward, ready to take on the guard, when Melissa flashed out of the corner of his eye.

The slight vampire dealt a sharp blow to the back of the guard's neck then proceeded to catch him when his eyes rolled back into his head.

Without a word she pulled the man behind the door before letting him drop, none too gently.

"Well, that was simple," she said, dusting off her hands.

A slow smile curved Tarian's lips. "I had it handled."

She shrugged. "I had it handled more. Are you going to go all he-man on me and tell me I should have waited for yet another rescue?"

Satisfaction filled him. "No," he replied. "I quite like that you don't need me to play your knight in shining armor at all times."

Her wide grin made him feel like he'd just said the exact right thing.

"Vampire males would have berated me for taking a risk."

"I'm not a vampire," he replied. How many times over the years had he protected someone who should have been able to do the job themselves? That would never be a worry with Melissa.

"So you don't mind that I might not need you all the time?"

He shrugged. "What sort of idiot would take issue with your ability to defend yourself?"

Her lips parted in surprise before joy washed over her features. Gripping his jacket, she pulled herself up on her tiptoes and kissed him.

Tarian groaned, knowing he should push her away. This wasn't the time or place. But Melissa had never made the first move before. His arms wrapped around her as he took one selfish minute to revel in her touch.

"We don't have time for this," he whispered against her lips.

"I know." She slid back down to the ground. "But tonight I think we should stop driving earlier."

It took his brain a moment to process what she'd just said. When he did, fire roared through his blood. "Yes?"

She nodded. "Provided we survive, of course."

"Oh sweetheart, you've just given me quite a powerful reason to live." With a last, quick kiss, he pushed her behind him and reached for the door.

The lobby spread out before them, empty of everyone except the boy on reception.

*Perfect,* he thought. They just needed to get out and find the car. Once they were on the road, Dominic wouldn't catch them twice.

Melissa's hands pressed against his back as she leaned forward to peer over his shoulder. Her scent wrapped around him, a mix of floral hotel shampoo and something uniquely her.

"Is it clear?" she whispered in his ear.

He bit back a growl. Escaping from his family with a damn hard-on had not been in the cards.

"Looks clear. We should—"

"Wait." Melissa's fingers curled into him. "There."

He saw exactly what had caused her to stop him. Dominic strode into view, his salt-and-pepper hair unmistakable.

Tarian glanced around the simple lobby and knew there was no way to escape without his grandfather spotting them.

"Any ideas?" she breathed into his ear.

He was about to say no when a second shape emerged from the hallway.

"Yes," he replied, power coursing through him. Usually he needed to be close to use his magic against his fellow necromancers, but desperate times called for desperate measures.

His eyes slid closed, tension knotting his shoulders, as he focused on the second guard. Magic flowed from him, caressing along Melissa's skin as it asked if she was the one meant to be influenced.

*Leave her alone,* he whispered to himself. *Trap the guard.*

Power flowed into the lobby, pooling around the hapless soldier.

When Tarian opened his eyes, he was seeing Dominic from a different angle.

"They've been spotted at the west end," he said, his voice rougher and deeper than it should have been.

Dominic turned to stare at him, or rather the guard. "Are you sure?" he demanded.

"Absolutely, sir. He still has the girl."

"Then let's go." Dominic took off down the hall, and Tarian pulled back his magic as the guard turned to do the same thing.

*West end,* he told the guard. *The traitor is hiding over there.*

Tarian stifled a groan as his magic boomeranged back into his body. Melissa was there, her arms wrapped around him in support.

"Want to tell me what just happened?" she asked.

"Later," he replied. By the time he got this vampire back to New York he'd have no secrets from her. The thought, however, wasn't as alarming as it would have been days past. "We need to run."

Catching her hand, he pulled her across the whitewashed floor toward the glass double doors.

Night had fallen by the time they burst from the hotel. A quick scan showed only two necromancers patrolling the parking lot. One more than he'd be able to control at once.

"Still want to show off your fancy vampire skills?" he asked.

Melissa glanced at him. "What were you thinking?"

"If you can incapacitate that one," he said, pointing to the furthest guard, "I can control the other."

"Deal." She was gone without another word.

Tarian watched in surprise as the guard he'd indicated went down in a soundless attack. He hadn't even seen her move. Vampires were deadly creatures, he'd seen that first hand, but Melissa's bloodthirstiness had a certain elegance that brought a smile to his face.

A smile that disappeared when she took down the second guard instead of staying hidden.

"Melissa," he hissed, racing across the parking lot.

He found her dragging the second guard next to the first.

"What?" she asked. "He didn't see his friend go down, so as long as I stayed on his blind side there was no chance of him controlling me."

The desire to shake her made his fingers twitch. "It was an unnecessary risk."

"It was my call," she snapped back. "And it went off without a hitch. The appropriate response is, 'Thank you my lovely, brilliant vampire. I'd be lost without you.'"

Staring at her grinning like a loon while kneeling next to two unconscious necromancers caused a curious pang to snake through him. He just might be lost without her.

"Come on," he said, unlocking the car. "Let's get out of here before Dominic realizes we're not in the west end of this place."

Melissa made no protest, and within minutes they were

jetting off onto the road.

"Think they'll be able to follow us?" Melissa asked. She turned to look back at the hotel, as it grew smaller in his rearview mirror.

"I'm sure Dominic won't be giving up, but we'll just stick to the smaller rural roads."

"How'd they find us this time?"

He shook his head, unable to answer her. Dominic had many talents but tracking wasn't one of them. "I have no idea," he said truthfully.

"Good thing you've got crazy, these-aren't-the-droids-you're-looking-for powers." She flopped back into her seat and fastened her eyes on him. "Let's talk about that, shall we?"

Tarian groaned. He'd never be able to convince her she hadn't seen what she'd seen, but the answers Melissa was searching for were ones he'd only intended to share with his mate.

*And that's not her,* he told himself. Fate wouldn't have been cruel enough to pair him with a woman he could never have. Not permanently.

And he wouldn't be stupid enough to fall for a vampire who was far too young and naive to ever be what he needed.

*It's just lust. We both just need a night to get each other out of our systems.*

Even as he assured himself, the words felt hollow. Tarian wasn't sure there was anything he could do to scrub Melissa from his mind.

Nor was he sure he even wanted to.

• • •

"Tarian?" she asked. The seriousness in his eyes was unnerving. What was running through his mind?

"Did it ever occur to you I wouldn't want to share all my innermost secrets with a woman I—"

He stopped, but she could fill in the blanks. With a woman he might never see again after tomorrow night.

Melissa turned to the window, her excitement over their escape fading away at the reality of their situation. She'd read the articles. Relationships between people brought together by stress or extreme circumstances rarely lasted. Added to that, they were both looking for their intended mates.

The idea of Tarian finding his, of smiling at some other woman, loving her, made her fangs ache. But there was no use hiding from the truth. Tarian wasn't hers. Their romance came with a time limit.

It didn't stop her from wanting to know him.

She leaned her head back against the seat rest. Never before had she felt obliged to share intimate details about herself with a partner, nor had she pried into a lover's past. She'd lived by the unspoken immortal rule that the past was off-limits for all but the most serious of connections.

Now, however, the idea of opening herself up to someone didn't fill her with the usual dread. Tarian wasn't a man she felt the need to keep at arm's length anymore. In fact, he was the first to ever inspire this desire to share.

She wanted to learn about his powers, but more so, she wanted to know about his life before he came into her world. It was selfish to expect such closely guarded secrets without offering up a few of her own.

"Quid pro quo," she whispered.

"What?"

She rolled her head in his direction. If she was going to go down this road it couldn't be brought on by a thoughtless blunder or a slip of the tongue. It had to be a conscious decision, because once they parted ways, the information they shared might come back to haunt them.

"I want to know you," she said, staring at his profile. "And I'll pay your price."

His hands tightened on the steering wheel. "I'll ask about your transformation," he warned.

"I know."

There was a beat of silence. "Vampires don't offer up that information to just anyone."

"Yes."

His eyes flicked to her. "This is a bad idea. Keeping our distance makes things easier."

"Much," she agreed. Not that she'd been very good at keeping her hands off him. Maintaining distance seemed to be a hopeless dream for them.

Tarian sighed before giving his head a rough shake. "Dammit. You've been a puzzle I've wanted to unravel since I bloody well met you."

A small smile curved her lips. At least she wasn't alone in this twisted dance they found themselves tangled in.

"Tell me," he ordered.

Her eyes closed briefly as the memory of screaming horses thundered in her mind. She was about to speak of a time in her life she tried her best to forget. The most painful night of her existence.

"I should have died in a carriage accident," she whispered. "The same accident that killed my mother."

His breath hissed from him. "Melissa—"

"No," she stopped him. "I think…I think I want to tell you."

Though his gaze didn't waver from the road, one hand reached out for hers.

"I never knew much about my biological father," she continued. "We didn't exactly live in a time period with alimony."

"Redgrave is not…?"

"No. He met my mother in a busy tavern and had to have her. I was just a child when they started their relationship."

Usually pain shot through her when she spoke of her past, but not this time. She thought of the accident without the usual shame she felt that she could barely remember her mother's face, even though she hadn't forgotten the warmth of her touch or the love in her voice.

As the silence stretched, Tarian offered her a respite.

"I was a strong necromancer from the time of my birth," Tarian said, his voice rough. "But my other powers developed over time. I can sense my kind, as you know, and sometimes I can command them as I would a vampire. It only works on the younger or weak willed of my kind, but I can do it."

She glanced at him. "Not Dominic."

"No. Not Dominic."

Necromancers shouldn't be able to control others of their kind. It was a talent she'd never even heard whispers about. That he'd trusted her with it gave her the courage to continue speaking of her transformation.

"My mother stayed with Lucian for the rest of her life," she said. "She loved him as she'd never loved another, but she refused to be transformed. She never wanted this life."

"Did she want it for you?"

Melissa closed her eyes, thinking back to the fateful day when her mortality had ended. "I don't know. She wanted me to live, though as what, I can only guess."

"What happened?"

"We were traveling to meet with Lucian. It was right at sunset and we were at the edge of a steep hill. Something spooked the horses, and the next thing I knew we were falling."

She still saw the rotating hill flash by her window in her nightmares. As they'd fallen, she'd seen her mother's terrified face. Both knew they weren't getting out alive.

"I was thrown free," she continued. "Hit my head and blacked out. Lucian tells me he raced to the scene as soon as the sun set but it was too late. I was unresponsive, and my mother was pinned under the carriage."

Tarian's hand tightened around hers. "The transformation can't heal extreme injuries."

"I know." The odds of her mother surviving even if she'd agreed to become a vampire were slim. Vampire blood had the power to heal almost any wound, but it still needed veins to circulate through. "She died making Lucian promise to take care of me. He would have anyway, but I like thinking that her last words were about me."

"So Lucian turned you."

"He wasn't going to risk losing us both. I didn't even get a choice, just woke up with an aversion to sunlight."

Tarian glanced at her. "Did you regret it?"

"No." Sometimes it made her feel guilty that she reveled in something he mother had loathed, but she loved her new life. Being a vampire, being strong and fast, gave her a power she'd never had as a human. Her mortal life would have been short and hard, but as an immortal she could enjoy the rolling of the years. She had experienced music, art, and culture that a normal lifespan would never have been able to offer. Even if Lucian had waited for her to wake before turning her, she wouldn't have made a different choice.

"Necromancers are born not turned," Tarian said. "We never have a choice."

"Did you want to be something else?"

A humorless smile twisted his lips. "For years. No necromancer child gives thanks for what we are. Not in a world that despises us."

Melissa looked away, knowing she'd been part of the world that had perpetuated anti-necromancer sentiments.

"Things changed during the wars. I was young and revolutionary."

"I doubt you were fighting for a world where necromancers and vampires were treated as equals."

He tensed. "No. I fought for the extinction of your kind."

She tried not to let the knowledge hurt. After all, Lucian had fought to eradicate necromancers, so fair was fair. Still, she couldn't help wondering if any trace of those hate filled years existed in the man she knew today.

"What changed your mind?"

"My father died. Killed by a vampire on the field. Suddenly it wasn't a game anymore."

"I'm sorry," she whispered.

Tarian shrugged. "It was a long time ago. My mother and I did our best to survive. She was always more of a pacifist than anyone else in the family."

"So you learned from her."

"Yes."

She smiled, cuddling up on her seat. "I'd like to meet her."

"She'd have liked you," Tarian replied. "But she died several decades ago."

The pit of her stomach dropped. Losing one parent was bad enough, but if anything happened to Lucian she wouldn't know how to exist.

"I'm sorry."

"We were in hiding, and she was pregnant. Hard to get good medical care when you have to avoid all the places decent doctors are likely to hang out."

Yet another reason to hate vampires.

"My sister survived," Tarian said. "And I had a reason to keep going."

"You had to protect her."

"Yes."

Melissa rested her head against the back of her seat. He'd lost his father in a war with her people. His mother had died because vampires used their influence to push his kind as far from the rest of the supernatural world as possible. Yet despite his past, he'd still faced off against what remained of his family in order to protect a kidnapped vampire.

"I don't understand why you don't hate me," she whispered. Anyone in his position should.

Tarian slammed on the brakes, swerving the car onto the shoulder of the road.

"Jeez, give warning much?" she squeaked as he reached for her. "Dominic will be after us."

"We lost him long ago, if he was ever following in the first place. Besides, this is more important."

"What is?"

"You." Sliding his seat back, he pulled her into his lap and wrapped his arms around her. "Not for a single moment have I hated you," he told her. "You had nothing to do with my sorry past."

"My people—"

"I don't think all vampires are evil, even if you think all necromancers are monsters."

She stiffened in his arms. "I don't…" her voice trailed off as the defense fell flat.

"We're your boogeymen," he replied. "No use denying it."

Twisting, she cupped his face between her hands. "That was before I met you."

"And now?" he breathed, his lips an inch from hers.

She stared into his beautiful eyes. He was reordering her world, making her question beliefs she'd never doubt- ed. Even worse, he filled her mind. Her waking hours were spent wondering about him, arguing with him, wanting him. Her daylight sleep spent dreaming of him. He was worming his way into every corner of her being, and the walls she'd built to keep him out were crumbling around their feet.

"Now?" she whispered, trailing her fingers along his strong jaw. "Now I'm finding I care less and less about what you are, so long as you're by my side."

As soon as the words were out she wanted to call them back. They were too revealing. Too pitiable. The last thing she wanted to be was the lonely vampire he'd once accused her of being. A few days and a couple heated embraces weren't enough to warrant such a declaration. She knew it as well as he. However, it didn't change the ever present need growing within her, not just to have him in her bed, but to have him in her life.

She focused on the curve of his collarbone. He was centuries older than her. Had lived experiences she could only dream of. No doubt her words sounded very young to him. And very naive.

"We should get going," she murmured, wanting to dispel her embarrassment. They'd go back to the road and talk of something light. Something that didn't reveal their pasts and further blur the line between ally and lover.

His fingers caught her chin as he gently forced her to raise her face. Knowing there was no help for it, she looked up and fell into his sapphire gaze. The world disappeared around them until she wasn't thinking of Dominic, or the wrath of her father. She wasn't thinking about saving lives or fighting prejudice.

The only thing on her mind was a burning desire to kiss him once more.

Their lips touched in a caress far more sweet than it was passionate. Tarian's hands slid down her back, holding her closer as his mouth slanted over hers. In her many years, she'd been kissed by more men than she could remember, but never had anyone touched her with such care. Her necromancer kissed her, and she felt treasured, precious.

*He's not mine,* she told herself. *Don't get used to this.* And she could. So easily. She could imagine herself fifty years from now, being calmed by his touch.

The universe had never been kind to her, but showing her such a perfect future only to snatch it away seemed particularly cruel.

His lips glided over hers before she felt the brush of teeth on her lower lip. A low moan caught in her throat. It seemed Tarian had adopted her penchant for love bites.

"Reckless," she said, tilting her head back so he could trail his mouth down her neck. "We should be driving."

"Tell me again," he replied.

She leaned back. "What?" she teased. "That you're slipping past all my best defenses?"

"Seems only fair. You've obliterated mine."

Her smile slipped from her face. The words might be light, but the meaning behind them was anything but. The embarrassment over her words drained away. It wasn't warranted. Not when he'd echoed the sentiment.

"What do we do?" she asked.

"What can we do?" he replied. "Other than drive fast and pull over early."

Her heart clenched. Unless some miracle happened, one night in his bed was all she'd ever get.

*Why am I surprised?* Her bad luck had run strong since the night her mother had died, when a five-minute delay in their accident would have had Lucian at their side.

"Okay," she agreed. "Let's drive fast." So she could enjoy her time with a man who had every cause to hate her, yet didn't. A man who had gone above and beyond to protect two races, without a word of thanks. A man who made her burn brighter than she could imagine her true mate ever would.

A man she'd be walking away from all too soon.

He helped her back into her seat before pulling onto the road. Melissa allowed the conversation to lag, knowing there was nothing more that needed to be said. For the first time, in a life filled with diplomacy and double talk, words were simply unnecessary.

# Chapter Twelve

Melissa stepped into the hotel room and flicked on the lights. This was the last night she'd have to sleep on sheets that smelled of astringent and shower with tiny bottles of formulaic body wash. Tomorrow she'd be back in her own bed.

Without Tarian.

She glanced back at her partner as he shut the door behind them.

"Are you hungry?" she asked. "We could get room service."

"No." He strode toward her. "At least, not hungry for food."

Heat flooded her at the lust in his expression. Melissa tamped down the butterflies in her stomach when he reached for her.

Tarian danced her into his arms to bring a smile to her face.

"You're far too serious," he murmured as he walked her backward toward the bed.

"Don't worry. Vampires can't get frown lines."

"Tomorrow you will be in the arms of your family."

She nodded. "And our alliance will be at an end."

"I'm not ready for that."

Melissa closed her eyes, knowing the feeling. "Me neither." But there was no delaying the inevitable. They needed to reach Lucian in time to plead Tarian's case.

"One last night," she whispered, looking up at him. "One last touch."

"Like this?" He trailed his fingers down her cheek.

"That's a little more subtle than I was thinking," she said. "I want more."

A soft smile flitted over his face. "From an enemy?"

She pressed her body against his. "I don't think that word has applied for a while now."

His lips claimed hers.

Melissa moaned as she twined her arms around his neck. One brush of his fingers and her panties were soaked through.

*This isn't wise,* her inner voice cautioned.

*Screw it,* she replied. She was this far down the rabbit hole. Might as well enjoy the madness.

Grabbing Tarian's shirt, she pulled him back toward the bed.

"We don't have to worry about the dawn this time," she said, her fingers skimming over his rock-hard erection.

Tarian hissed through his teeth. "Melissa…"

"Don't start something I can't finish?" she said. "Short of a group of zealous necromancers descending on this hotel room, nothing is going to stop me."

He raised his head to meet her gaze.

"I don't care," she whispered, seeing the question in his eyes. "What happens next, what we are to each other… I don't care. For once in my life, can't I just leap?"

"Yes," he replied. "I'm here to catch you."

His arms wrapped around her waist and lifted her off the floor. Laughter bubbled up in her throat as he tossed her onto the motel bed.

Melissa righted herself, bouncing on the mattress.

"What are you waiting for?" she asked, crawling back onto the center of the bed.

"Not a single thing."

Tarian gripped his shirt and tugged it over his head in one easy motion.

*Hot*, she thought, licking her lips in anticipation. She'd battled her desires for days and now here he was. No barriers, no pretenses. Her golden opportunity.

"Quid pro quo, right?" she asked, rising to her knees. Gripping her shirt, she pulled the cheap polyester over her head.

"More," he replied, staring straight at her breasts.

Melissa dragged a teasing finger along the rim of her bra. "If you want this gone," she murmured, pulling down on the lace to give him a peak of a nipple. "Then you need to lose another piece of clothing."

"Women have an unfair advantage in this game," he said, pushing the denim of his jeans over his hips.

She smoothed her triumphant smile with a hand. "Looking good, Tarian."

He stood before her in only his boxers. "Bra," he

demanded. "Off."

Obligingly, Melissa reached around for the clasp. Parting the metal hooks, she wiggled out of the confining contraption.

Tarian had no words as he stared at her, bared from the waist up.

A moment of hesitation hit her, since she didn't have the chest to rival most immortals. She didn't have the curves that brought men to their knees. Glancing down at her small breasts, she tried to muster her moxie. If he wanted this to go any further, then he had better think she was incredible, despite the handicap her immortality imposed on her.

"Seven hundred years," he said, his gaze locked on her. "And you are still the most beautiful thing I've ever seen."

The honesty in his voice warmed her. Her doubts melted away under the complete acceptance in his gaze. It didn't matter what issues she had about her body; to him she was perfect. And for the first time in her life, she was beginning to feel that way.

"Come to me," she said, reaching out to him.

He crawled onto the bed and hooked a hand around each ankle.

Melissa gasped as he tugged her flat onto her back. Her fingers flew to the clasp on her jeans and quickly undid the few buttons keeping her clothed.

With heated eyes, Tarian stripped the denim from her body.

"I think you missed something," she teased, wiggling backward in only her black silk underwear.

"Luckily, I'm a man who knows how to correct his mistakes." Gripping her panties, he tore the loose binding around her hips.

Melissa glanced at her ruined underwear with only mild regret. "You realize I'll have to go commando tomorrow."

His pupils dilated at the thought. "I'll never be able to drive us where we're going," he said. "Not when I know all I have to do is reach over and…"

Melissa caught his questing hand as it inched up her thigh. "Not so fast," she taunted.

"No?" He stood back against the side of the bed. "I guess it's only fair." He shed his boxers and Melissa's mouth went dry.

She'd known Tarian was muscled and hard in every area, but the sight of his cock jutting proudly from his body made her want to lick her lips. *Hers.* For tonight at least. She'd be damned if she wouldn't make it count.

"Come here," she said, holding out her arms to him.

Tarian wasted no time crawling back onto the bed. The mattress dipped under his weight as he leaned into her waiting arms.

Melissa lay flat against the sheets, looking up at him. As much as she'd dreamed of this moment, she'd never really expected to experience it in real life.

Her fingers rose to trace over his cheekbones, examining him with a gentle touch.

"Beautiful," she breathed. In every way. Tarian satisfied all the requirements she'd once set out for a mate.

"That's my line," he said, as his mouth touched hers.

Closing her eyes, she gave herself up to the pleasure of his touch. His mouth dragged along her in a sensual caress that had her moaning for more. Parting her lips, she met his questing tongue with her own.

Their panting breaths mingled as Melissa hooked a leg

over his hip. She undulated against him, pressing her breasts up against his hard chest.

His hands caressed down her sides, sliding over her hips as he explored the smooth lines of her legs. Melissa raked her nails down his chest, keeping her touch light enough to tantalize but not to hurt.

That she had the right to touch him in any way she saw fit filled her with a raw power she'd never felt before. One hand dipped low to brush against his erection, and she smiled at his swift inhale.

"Did I do something you like?" she asked, wrapping her fingers around his hard cock.

Melissa captured his lower lip between her teeth as she pumped her fist over his erection. Every moan that escaped him spurred her on. Tarian could control her with a thought, but right then, she was the one with the power. She couldn't stop her grin.

"Vixen," Tarian murmured. Grabbing her hands, he pressed them over her head.

Melissa tugged against her pinned hands. His strength held her in place, but they both knew she could tear free if she wanted. Score one for vampire advantage. "Don't you want to see what I can do with my tongue?" she taunted, arching her back to thrust her breasts up for his view.

"Yes," Tarian panted. "But not quite yet."

His hands left her wrists as his mouth kissed its way down her torso.

"Tarian," she breathed when his lips ran over her navel.

But he dipped lower. Heated hands pressed against her thighs, forcing them wider apart as he ducked between them.

The first lick of his tongue along her slit nearly sent her

rocketing from the bed.

Pleasure swamped her senses as he moved higher to encircle her clit.

"Yes," she cried as he wrung waves of delight from her willing body.

One hand joined his expert mouth. He teased a single finger along her folds as he took her clit into his mouth.

Melissa reached out to fist her hands in the sheets around her. The light scrape of teeth against the most sensitive nub on her body left her gasping with pleasure. When one finger stroked into her, she was beyond words.

Her fingers tangled in his hair as she fought not to press him forcefully against her. He drove a single digit into her while his tongue tortured a response from her. There was no stopping the helpless pleas that escaped her lips. Though her body craved a more complete release, she struggled not to rock against his mouth.

"Tarian," she gasped. "More."

Her lover left her with one last lick before climbing her body.

"Ready?" he asked, grinning down at her.

"I'll pay you back for that," she vowed, reaching up for him.

"I look forward to it." He reached down to adjust himself and Melissa felt the head of his cock press against her slit.

He drove into her without another word, and she threw her head back in pleasure. When he sat fully lodged within her, she fought to come to terms with the new feeling of fulfillment. Tarian stretched her to the limit, but he gave her time to get used to him, even as his muscles tensed and his breath came in shallow gasps.

Melissa wiggled, only to be rewarded by a bitten back curse.

"Again," he panted.

She was more than happy to oblige.

Tarian gripped her hips and withdrew to the tip before surging back into her.

Melissa planted her feet squarely on the bed as he rocked into her. The changed angle forced him even deeper in to her, wringing gasps of pleasure from her lips.

She wrapped one leg around his hips to urge him forward. Again and again she lifted her pelvis to meet his thrusts.

*More,* she begged, unsure whether the cry had left her mouth or merely echoed in her mind. Every movement within her spiked a sensation unlike any she'd known before.

They writhed together, straining to find completion. Melissa felt her orgasm pulling at her, demanding just a little more. Just another stroke.

Her teeth scraped against his skin as she fought the urge to drive her fangs into his neck.

"Do it," he groaned.

It was all the permission she needed.

Melissa bit down. Blood washed over her tongue as Tarian thrust wildly within her. Every sensation, every touch, was heightened. Her body clenched around him even as she tried to match his desperate speed.

She swallowed the rich blood as he drove back into her, and her world shattered. Waves of pure pleasure buffeted her. Melissa heard Tarian cry out as his climax claimed him, felt the hot seed spurt into her, but his satisfaction only added to her own release.

Melissa thrashed as the sensations crashed over her. She clutched Tarian tight, as her anchor in the storm. Even when the tingles of pleasure started to fade, she refused to release her grip on him.

Luckily he seemed to share her affliction. His arms wrapped around her, holding her close as she took one last pull on his throat.

"Amazing," she purred, lapping her tongue over the tiny puncture wounds.

"Seconded," he panted as he rolled to his side.

She snuggled against him, closing her eyes in utter contentment. Sleeping with him was supposed to have gotten him out of her system, but she feared their tryst would have the opposite effect. How did she give up the best sex of her life?

Trailing her fingers lightly over his chest, she knew she was well and truly stuck. *Can't let him go, can't find a way to keep him.* What was she supposed to do?

In the absence of an answer, she merely watched her lover's happy face and wished, just this once, that the night would never end.

# Chapter Thirteen

"Maybe I should face him alone."

Tarian arched a brow. "You think he's not going to open the door the second he hears the elevator?"

"You can stay inside."

"Or I can face your father and try to stop him from going after my people."

Melissa shifted from foot to foot, staring at the rising numbers above the door. "Promise not to use your voodoo on him?"

"No."

She hadn't been nervous in years, but the moment they crossed into the city limits, her blood pressure had shot through the roof. Well…if she had blood pressure. But the feeling had been similar. Introducing her father to the man that was indirectly responsible for her kidnapping was not going to be an easy ride. Especially when said man was also her lover. The last time she'd brought a partner home had been in the early thirties, and watching him run as fast as he could from her door had been great incentive not to repeat the experience.

"Remember," Tarian said as the numbers climbed toward the top floor. "What happens from here on out is not about us."

"We just have to calm the waters," she agreed. Even so, she stepped into his arms and inhaled his scent. After the night they'd shared, she couldn't imagine letting him walk away from her. If she had to fight her father to keep him, she would.

A small ding signaled the end of their journey.

Rolling her shoulders back, she stepped into the tasteful hallway that boasted an apartment at each end.

Just as Tarian predicted, the door to her father's penthouse was open.

"Thank you," she whispered to Tarian. "No matter what happens."

He caught her arm and pressed his lips to hers. "All's not lost yet, sweetheart."

Giving him a last smile, she strode through the open door.

Inside was exactly as she'd expected. Lucian paced the length of the living room while Abbey sat curled up on the sofa looking worried.

"Hi," she called, feeling both uncertainty and longing at the same time.

Both Lucian and Abbey swung toward her. Abbey's face drained of blood before a wide grin curved her lips.

"Melissa," she said like a prayer, pushing from her seat.

Lucian was faster. Using vampire speed, he crossed the

room to her in an instant.

"You're safe?" he demanded, looking her up and down.

"I'm fine," she replied.

"Good."

She was pulled into a tight hug before she could get out another word. Instead of protesting, she closed her eyes and hugged her father back. How many times since her ordeal began had she wanted to simply wrap her arms around him and listen to him promise that everything would be all right?

It was lucky she didn't need to breathe or Lucian's grip would have crushed her. She was only saved when Abbey caught up with them and elbowed Lucian out of the way.

"Abbey, it's good to—*oomph.*" Her words were cut off as her friend wrapped her in an equally tight embrace.

"We thought we'd never see you again," Abbey babbled in her ear. "Those first two days were torture."

She wrapped her arms carefully around the human and returned the hug. Abbey had not been in her life as long as Lucian, but she'd become equally as dear. Though the woman would one day technically be her stepmother, Melissa had waited decades for a friend like her.

"I'm sorry," she said. "I would never have left you of my own volition."

"Precisely," Lucian said. "Which is why we will crush whoever took you."

Melissa shook free of Abbey and faced off against her father. "You need to listen to me first."

"All I need to do is get the relevant details before I contact the council," he replied. "We'll bring those who took you to justice."

"That's where I come in." Tarian stepped through the

door, hands in his pockets.

Lucian bared his teeth as he lunged for the necromancer.

"No," Melissa shouted, jumping in front of Tarian. "You will sit and you will listen, Father, or I will march out the door with Tarian."

"I knew it," Abbey murmured.

"I can smell the necromancer blood in him," Lucian growled. "You brought one of his kind into my home."

"I did," she agreed. "Because he saved my life, and you need to listen to what he has to say."

Lucian's gaze flicked from her to Tarian. "Saved your life how?"

"He wasn't among the group who kidnapped me."

"The date—"

"Look," she said. "Let's not stand here in the entryway like scrabbling children. At the very least we can talk about this like civilized adults."

*Civilized adults that have been trying to kill each other for most of the millennia,* she amended, as she shooed them down the few stairs into the open concept living room. Abbey followed her directions by plopping down into an overstuffed armchair while Lucian stood over her. Given the vampire's refusal to sit, Tarian also stayed on his feet, moving so the wide windows were at his back.

Melissa sighed, running a hand down her face. "Okay, here's the deal. Yes, I was kidnapped by necromancers but they are a small faction that do not represent the majority of their kind." Lucian snorted but she talked over him. "Tarian risked both his life and his family ties to come get me. He snuck me out of the necromancer property and kept us off their radar as we drove home. Right from the start, his only goal was to get me back here, safe and sound."

"Why?" Lucian demanded. "What was his motive?"

"To keep an innocent from harm," Tarian snapped.

"Even if that innocent has fangs? I very much doubt it."

"Just because you are blinded by your own prejudice doesn't mean I am."

Lucian snarled. "You will show me some respect, boy."

"Only when you earn it, leech," Tarian said with a derisive laugh.

Before Melissa could diffuse the situation, her father launched himself at Tarian. With a cry she rushed forward only to pause when her lover threw out a hand.

Lucian stopped in midstep, his clawed hands raised, fangs glistening.

Tarian's eyes were cold as he stepped toward the immobile man. "You might do well to remember you're not the top of the evolutionary chain, vampire," he hissed. "I am."

"Tarian, let my father go," Melissa ordered.

His gaze flicked her way before returning to Lucian. "You, I promised immunity," he said to her. "No one else."

"You can't kept that up forever. Please."

The entire room waited in silence to see how he would respond to her entreaty. Finally he flicked his fingers. Lucian stumbled forward a step as control returned to his body.

The vampire bared his fangs, which had Tarian raising his hand in warning.

A soft chuckle broke the tension.

"They always say girls date their fathers," Abbey laughed. "My god, Melissa. You didn't branch out much."

Three sets of incredulous eyes swung to her.

"Abbey," Lucian reproved.

Ignoring him, Abbey focused on Melissa and ticked off her points on her fingers. "Old as the hills. Powerful. Has a temper. Ruthless in defense of those he loves. Hot, and, forgive me, but I'm assuming one hell of a lover, if you brought him here."

"Aw…ick," Melissa said, pressing her hands over her ears. "Abbey, really."

The human shrugged. "Am I wrong?"

Tarian and Lucian eyed each other.

"I do not see your basis for comparison," Lucian said.

"Ah, honey. I know you don't." Abbey grinned up at him.

In typical Lucian fashion, her father chose to focus on the one fact in Abbey's speech she'd rather he not.

"Are you lovers?" he demanded.

Tarian drew up in affront even as Melissa sprang to the rescue. "That is not your business."

"Given his bloodline, it most certainly is." He caught her arm and pulled her to the side. "Our kind are vulnerable to his. How do you know he did not take advantage of the situation?"

"That's it," Tarian said, shaking out his hands. "I haven't killed a vampire in decades, but this seems as good a time as any to dust off old skills."

"Stop," she growled at him in exasperation. "Lucian, I spent four nights with this man and he did nothing but keep me safe. Doesn't that tell you something?"

"He knew the exact best way to get into your pants?" her friend piped up.

Melissa shot a death glare at Abbey. "Not helpful."

The other woman shrugged. "Honestly, I'm not sure what side I should be on."

"Not all necromancers are evil," she said, facing Lucian. "This one group that kidnapped me, sure. But Tarian risked a lot to come to my rescue. Are you going to vilify him for that?"

"He could have had you call me the second you were safe," Lucian replied. "Drake knew what he was about when he kept you by his side for these past nights."

"It would have put her in danger," Tarian said. "My grandfather's reach is wide. He would have stopped her from boarding a plane."

"I have resources your grandfather doesn't," Lucian snapped. "Melissa would have been perfectly safe."

"Are you willing to bet her life on it? Because I wasn't."

Lucian leveled an icy glare at him. "I would have kept her from harm."

"I *did*," he argued.

"And what do you want for it, hmm? What's your price for returning Melissa unharmed?"

"It's not like that," she tried, even as Tarian spoke.

"Clemency for the necromancer community," he said. "We are not all in support of violence to settle our score. I propose we meet with the council and review the terms of the necromancer ban. My people are suffering, and yours are the cause."

Melissa flinched. This had always been the plan, but even so, it hurt to hear him claim that protecting her was just to achieve his goals, not because he cared.

"There we are," Lucian said, tension leaving his shoulders. "The heart of the matter." He glanced at Abbey before shaking his head. "Because my daughter obviously cares for you—just as I'm sure you guaranteed would be the case—I will make you a deal." When he turned back to Tarian, Melissa flinched at his intractable expression. "I will vow no vengeance for Melissa's abduction against any part of the necromancer community, provided you return to your shadows. There is no room for you here in New York."

"That is not enough. If you don't at least think about making changes, this unrest will never end."

"This is all I'm offering. Refuse and I will happily tear your head from your shoulders before hunting down every last necromancer I can find."

"Lucian," Melissa tried to protest.

"No." He silenced her with a wave of his hand. "This is about more than you and your boyfriend. I will not endanger the vampires of this city."

"We only want peace," Tarian growled.

"And you have nothing to bargain with. Take my offer, and leave my home."

Tarian's shoulders stiffened. "You swear neither you, nor the council, will come after any faction of our society?"

"My word," Lucian agreed.

Tarian's eyes met hers, and she read the resignation in them. No matter that he was in the right, the vampire community held all the cards.

"Father, that's not fair," she tried to cut in.

"I'll deal with you later, Melissa," Lucian replied. "But right now I am speaking as the elder of the vampire race, not as your father."

"Lucian…" Abbey tried. "Think carefully about this. Is Tarian's request so out of bounds?"

"Take it or leave it," he told Tarian. "With one phone call I can rally an army against your people. And the first place I'll start is with the woman in your home."

Tarian's shoulders bowed. "I accept," he said, disdain dripping from his words.

"Good. Then there is just one more condition you need to agree to in order to ensure immunity for your people." Lucian's gaze turned to her. "You will say goodbye to my daughter and never contact her again. If you do so, I will retract my promise to leave the necromancers alone."

"No," Melissa cried. "You can't do this. I'm not a child you need to save anymore."

"You will always be my child," he replied. "And I will always protect you. Even if it's from yourself."

Abbey pushed to her feet. "Lucian, this is exactly what I was talking about. You can't control who she cares about."

"Perhaps not. But I can keep the damned necromancer away from her, where he can't continue to blind her with infatuation." He looked back to Tarian. "Do we have a deal, or should I make my call?"

Melissa met Tarian's tortured gaze and knew how this night would end. They'd suspected, of course, but planning for a lonely future and facing it were two different things.

"Please don't do this," she said to Lucian, without taking her eyes off her lover.

"I have no other choice," he replied. "Not when it comes to your safety."

Tarian's expression blanked. "I accept. I will leave New York at once and never come back."

"And what if I go with him?" Melissa demanded, rounding on her father. "What if I give up my life here and follow him?"

"Then I will consider his bargain null and void and go

after the necromancers who took you."

"Melissa."

She turned to find Tarian at her side. He took her hands and pulled her close, ignoring the growl that rumbled from Lucian's chest. "We knew it would turn out this way."

"No," she denied. "We can reason with him. I can change his mind."

A tiny smile curved his lips. "You are a powerful, capable woman, sweetheart. But I doubt even you are capable of that."

Her hands tightened on his. "I can't say goodbye to you."

Tarian closed his eyes as he leaned his forehead against hers. "Thank you," he whispered.

A sob caught in her throat. "I did nothing. Less than nothing."

"I didn't lie when I said I no longer hated your kind, but neither did I exactly care for the vampire population." His hands transferred to her waist, pulling her close. "But you changed all that."

"How?" she asked, her voice little more than a breathless sigh.

"When I look at you, sweetheart, I see the woman behind the fangs. One who I will never forget. One who matters more than you will ever know."

She closed her eyes, feeling a suspicious moisture gather behind her lids. "I don't want to say goodbye."

"Eternity is a long time. We might meet again."

It was cold comfort when her arms would be empty tonight.

"I—" But she couldn't say the words her heart cried. It was too soon. And too cruel. He didn't need such a burden when walking away from her.

"I know," he breathed, his voice almost too soft for her supernatural hearing. "Have a happy life, Melissa. Find your mate."

*I already found him,* she wanted to scream, but instead she nodded. "Goodbye, Tarian. Be safe."

He pressed his lips to her forehead, a mockery of the kiss she truly craved, before stepping past her. Tarian didn't pause as he walked out of the door and out of her life.

Melissa waited in silent pain as her ears heard the sound of the elevator doors close behind him.

Only then did she turn to her father.

"I will never forgive you for this," she vowed.

He looked at her with bleak eyes as he inclined his head. "I know."

Turning on her heel, she marched away from the family she'd spent days trying to reach.

# Chapter Fourteen

"There's a walk-in for you, Ms. Redgrave."

Melissa glanced up from her desk. "I have a few minutes, Mary. As long as the issue isn't too pressing, show them in."

She turned back to her computer screen, staring sightlessly at the plans for the museum fundraiser she'd once been so excited about. But that had been B.T.D. Before Tarian Drake. Life after him seemed far more colorless than it ever had before. Her charities and responsibilities were monotonous. For all of the difference she was making in the human world, she had zero power in the supernatural one.

"Melissa?"

The soft voice had her head shooting up. Abbey stepped through the doorway, crossing to her desk as she had a hundred times before.

"Don't," Melissa warned as she sat.

"It's been a week," she said. "Time to come out of mourning."

"Oh really?" She arched a brow. "How long were you laid up the first time Lucian dumped you?"

Abbey flinched, and for a moment she regretted the harsh words. Her friend was not the real target of her anger.

"As you point out, I'm no stranger to loss," Abbey began.

"Temporary loss," Melissa cut her off. "We can't trade war stories until Lucian walks away from you and never looks back." An impossibility, and they both knew it.

"Lucian is my mate," Abbey tried. "It wouldn't be the same."

She turned back to her computer and refused to look at her friend.

"I'm sure Tarian was adventurous and fun, but he wasn't your mate," Abbey said.

Silence stretched while she refused to comment.

"Was he?" Abbey breathed.

A growl caught in her throat. "I don't know," she nearly snarled. "My father ruined any chance of finding that out."

"But...it's so fast."

"You are the relationship expert. Tell me how long mates normally take to recognize each other."

"Two to three months," she said in reply. "Though not all matches follow that time frame."

"What was the fastest you have on record?"

Abbey chewed her lip before relenting. "Twelve hours."

Melissa snorted. "Sounds like time doesn't really factor into this then, does it?"

"Fair point. But Melissa, if he was your mate, you'd be bleeding right now." Abbey drew a deep breath. "When Lucian left me it was like the color left the world. I know humans view mating differently than you do, but the devastation would be the same. So the question remains, is that how you are feeling?"

She turned away, unwilling to confess anything to a woman who would only report back to her father.

Abbey waited a long moment before pulling something from her bag.

"You got a 94 percent match," she said, tossing the folder onto the desk. "I told you Vivian was running a recruitment campaign, and it actually worked. We had a flood of new members in the past few days. There are a few others I could set you up, with but none as high as him."

Melissa flipped the beige folder open and looked down at the print out of a member's match profile.

"Gryphon," she said.

"Strong. Handsome. No baggage. He's not likely to abduct you before a date."

"Neither did Tarian."

Abbey waved the protest away. "Semantics."

Melissa snapped the file closed. "I'm not interested."

"A match that high is unheard of."

She refrained from hissing at her friend. "Did I push you to date when you were abandoned?"

"I believe there was some talk about getting back on the horse, yes."

Shame shot through her. "Then I'm sorry. That was insensitive of me."

"You are really taking this hard," Abbey said, surprise on her face.

Melissa picked up the file and held it out to her. "I'm not interested in any matches. I realize I have four more handpicked dates left, but I really don't care. Please put my account on hold for the time being."

"On hold? Are you sure?"

"Yes," she replied. "As much fun as pretending not to be heartbroken sounds, I'd prefer to stick my hand in sunlight."

"Melissa," Abbey reproved.

"My point," she stressed, "is that unless you are here to tell me Lucian has allowed Tarian to see me without endangering a whole society of people you need to leave."

"I might be Lucian's mate, but I'm your friend," she protested.

"Exactly. If forced to choose, which way do you fall?" Abbey looked away, and Melissa smiled darkly. "I rest my case."

"So that's it? Lucian and I never hear from you again?"

She fell back against her chair. "I don't know," she answered truthfully. "But I'm done with being treated like a child, and he won't see me any other way."

"Maybe we can work on that."

"He's got three bodyguards shadowing my every move. Did he think I wouldn't notice?"

Abbey sighed. "I told him not to do that."

"Try harder next time."

"He's just worried."

"Why?" Melissa demanded. "He chased off the only man I've been serious about in years. I'm well into cat-buying mode by now."

"Be serious."

"You think I'm not? Not only are they great companions, they're fantastic substitutes for those late nights when you just don't feel like hunting."

"Seriously?" Abbey asked with a shudder.

"Look, my point is, both of you need to back off. While I have no issue with you per se, you come attached to a man I'd rather not see for a few decades, and if Lucian has an issue with that then he'll just have to deal. It's his actions that landed us here in the first place."

"He did what he thought was best."

"He failed. Now, I have a midnight appointment with the curator of the Met. I'm sure you can see yourself out."

Abbey sighed as she rose. "We're still family, Melissa."

"For millennia to come," she agreed. "This might make for great family reminiscences three hundred years from now, but not today. Tell Lucian to back off, or I will move to Europe and he won't see me for a century."

"I'll pass it on," she agreed, but not before she rounded the table and hugged Melissa with an awkward one armed embrace. "I'm here if you need me."

Melissa watched her walk from the office and wished she could demand she make Lucian change his mind. Tarian would have to give two weeks notice at his work, but after that he'd be gone and beyond her reach. She might never be able to track him down again. After all, one thing necromancers were good at was disappearing.

• • •

He needed to vanish.

Tarian paced through the downstairs, checking in each room. "Eilin?" he called. Where was that girl?

His real estate agent had called today with an offer for the house. He only needed a few more days to tie up his position, and then he'd be free of the city. Eilin had been less than impressed with the news they had to move again, but he'd refrained from pointing out that it was, at least in part, her fault.

"I've got an offer on the house we should discuss," he called up the stairs. His sister had been avoiding him for days, but he hadn't begrudged her the solitude. Actually, it had made things simpler. Far easier to hide a broken heart when no one was watching.

*Not a broken heart,* he told himself once again. He'd have to love Melissa for that to be the case, and a few days in her presence weren't enough to convince him she was the woman he'd waited lifetimes to find.

Of course, his previous lovers hadn't haunted his dreams after the relationship ended. They hadn't consumed his every waking thought. All he had to do was close his eyes, and he remembered the desolate look on Melissa's face as he'd walked away.

*She is not your concern,* he thought. In order to protect his people, he could never see her again.

Even if he ached to.

"Eilin," he called again, running up the stairs. The silent treatment was getting old. His sister was in her eighties, not her teens, and though moving was a hassle, she needed to help with this process.

"I'm coming in," he said, knocking on her door. Opening it, he glanced into the empty room. Eilin was nowhere to be seen, and her queen bed was neatly made, as if no one had slept in it. With a frown he shut the door and searched the rest of the floor. Not only was she not in her room, she wasn't anywhere.

The doorbell rang before real worry could set in. Eilin

had given her word she wouldn't leave the house, and he still had the basement to check.

"Coming," he called as he jogged down the steps. Wherever his sister was hiding he'd find her and force her into a decent conversation with him. They needed to plan their next steps. His drive through Oklahoma had endeared him to the state, but he still needed her input before he uprooted their entire lives and picked a new spot.

Tarian yanked open the door and regretted it instantly.

"Hello, Tarian," Dominic said.

"You are not welcome here."

"I suspected as much." He pushed past Tarian and into the hall. "Despite the fact it was my money that purchased this land for your mother."

"She wanted nothing to do with you," he said. "You know that."

Dominic glanced back at him before prowling deeper into the house. "Yes. I know very well, Tarian."

He shut the door as he debated his options. As much as he'd like to denounce the man, Dominic still shared his blood. He could call the vampires, but Lucian would just label him as guilty as his grandfather was.

"What do you want?" he asked, pacing after Dominic.

He found his grandfather standing in the family room, looking out at the sunny space with smiling pictures of Eilin and himself framing the walls.

"You tried to make a home here," Dominic said, walking past the worn gray sofa and cluttered coffee table.

"It would have worked had you left well enough alone."

"Ah yes. You'd have the house, the job..." He glanced back at Tarian. "The girl."

"We're moving," Tarian said. "In a few days. You're to thank for that."

"Had you not ruined our plans, this could have been your permanent home."

"Not even for this house was your plan reasonable."

Dominic scoffed as he leaned forward to study the pictures. "You never let me know her," he said, studying a smiling photo of Eilin.

"You had contact by phone."

"But few visits. My own granddaughter."

"It was all you needed to seduce her to your way of thinking. I shudder to think how brainwashed she'd be if I'd let you any closer."

"Not brainwashed," Dominic corrected. "She wanted to fight for our people. For our cause."

Tarian shook his head in disgust "And that's all you cared about. Creating another soldier for your war. There isn't a paternal bone in your body."

"It would have been nice to know I was leaving the community in good hands should anything happen to me."

"I promise, should you disappear, it will be in far better hands."

"Those of a pacifist?" Dominic asked, glancing at him. "You are my heir, Tarian, and you've never had the stomach for blood."

"Not past the fifteenth century, no."

"I tried to convince your mother not to coddle you. She was so distraught after her husband's death."

"Mate," he hissed. "She lost her mate and still managed to survive him for centuries."

"Makes you wonder how strong the bond was, doesn't

it?" Dominic asked, turning to face him. "She found a replacement for your father, something a truly mated woman should never have been capable of."

His hands clenched into fists but he refused to get pulled into the argument. Whatever his parents' relationship, it was all in the past.

"Whatever she was, she was clear about her desire to separate from you," Tarian said.

For a second he could have sworn pain flashed across Dominic's face. "Yes. She hid you for centuries. Always moving. Always avoiding the conflict. But then Eilin came into the picture." Dominic clasped his hands behind his back. "Quite the little revolutionary you've raised, Tarian. Did you know she walked into my car without much prompting at all?"

Ice ran down his spine. "What?"

"I have Eilin," Dominic said, moving away from the pictures. "And I can see so much of your mother in her. It would be a shame if anything were to happen."

Tarian shook his head, resisting the urge to rend flesh before he fully understood the situation. "You took Eilin? Why?"

"Because you have direct access to the woman I really want."

"Melissa."

"Melissa," Dominic agreed. "I'm quite happy to trade, of course. Once I have the vampire, you and Eilin can go wherever you wish. I promise not to contact you again. I can do that much in the memory of my poor daughter."

"But protecting her children doesn't count as honoring her memory?"

"Not if it conflicts with my plans," Dominic said, his eyes hard. "We both have something the other wants. Honestly, Tarian, even with your peaceful views this should be an easy call. After all, it's not like the vampire is your mate." He laughed at the notion.

"You wouldn't hurt your own flesh and blood," Tarian said, ignoring the digs.

"Oh, I assure you, in order to help our people I would rip both you and Eilin to shreds, if I thought it was necessary." He shrugged. "Luckily it is only a vampire I need."

"I don't have access to her anymore."

"You'll figure it out." Dominic tossed him a burner phone. "You can contact me via that line. Call me as soon as you have the vampire to exchange, and I'll meet you with Eilin. This doesn't need to be any harder than you make it, Tarian."

"Eilin trusted you," he said. "She loved the idea of having a grandfather out there, even if he wasn't with her."

"She's young," Dominic said with no inflection. "She'll learn not to be such a fool in the future."

"I won't ever forgive you for this. Neither will she."

Dominic strode forward and clapped a hand on his shoulder. "I don't need your forgiveness," he said. "I need your lover."

He walked past Tarian and down the hallway.

"Call me when you are ready to exchange," he said. "And don't keep me waiting. For Eilin's sake."

The door closed behind him on the way out.

Tarian stood in the empty family room and looked at the framed pictures of his sister. No matter what happened, he was not sacrificing her for family ambition.

Which meant he needed a vampire. One whom he'd walked away from.

He ran his fingers through his hair. Eilin had to come first. She was his sister. His family.

Melissa was just…

With a growl he slammed his fist into the wall. Plaster puffed into the air as larger chunks rained down on his shoes.

He'd done everything in his power to keep Melissa safe, but the game had changed now. The choices were different. He refused to leave Eilin in Dominic's clutches.

Which left one option.

Cold resolve filled him as he straightened. No matter his feelings, Eilin had to come first. Melissa wasn't his family. She wasn't his mate.

Right now, she was simply a means to an end.

And he had no choice but to use her.

# Chapter Fifteen

She flicked the lights on the moment she stepped through her apartment door and let out a long sigh. Her job seemed far more boring than she'd remembered it, tonight especially. Thankfully she'd managed to take a half-night and come home for some R and R.

Kicking off her Louboutins, she left them by the door without a second glance. The thought of a mug full of bagged blood didn't put a skip in her step, but as least it would satisfy the rumbling in her stomach.

Heading down the hallway to her kitchen she passed by the living room and froze.

Someone sat in the dark room, looking out her patio window at the city below.

Claws lengthened from her fingernails as she crept into the room. If this was a necromancer, she didn't want to give them any warning of her attack.

"The thing about having vampire guards," Tarian's voice

said, breaking through the darkness. "Is that they are very easy to manipulate, if you have the right touch."

"Tarian," she breathed.

He turned to face her.

"Hello, Melissa."

Relief rushed through her. Her first instinct was to run across the room and throw herself into his arms. She made it halfway across the living room before the hard edge to his voice registered. Pausing, she raked her gaze over her lover. Gone were the casual jeans and plaid he'd had to wear during their road trip. In their place was an immaculate black suit. Power crackled in the air, twining around his rigid form. As much as she wanted to hold him, something wasn't right.

"What's happened?"

"Dominic's in town."

She stiffened. "Impossible."

"Oh, I promise you, reason does not dissuade my grandfather." He stepped around the armchair into the center of the room.

He looked wildly out of place in her staid, minimalist living room, standing between the glass coffee table and beige couch. As it was, she could barely believe she was seeing him again, even if the circumstances were less than ideal. If her heart could beat, it'd be racing out of her chest.

"What does he want?" she asked, trying to play this as cool as he was.

"You, of course. And this time he's decided to up his game."

"How?" Though her body burned for his touch, she still retreated a step when he prowled toward her. The look on his face reminded her of the night he'd walked into

Dominic's ranch house and interrupted their dinner. He'd been a stranger to her then. A man tied to a dangerous past.

"He's recruited me."

Melissa swallowed. "You would never help him."

"Which he knows. So he took my sister."

"Damned man only has one go-to move."

He stopped in front of her, watching her with his icy gaze. "He'll only exchange her for you. So tell me, Melissa, what would you do in my place?"

She hesitated, flexing her hands to shake out the tingle of her claws edging toward the surface. The man before her was a far sight from the lover she'd laughed with. Tarian was caught between a rock and a hard place and looking for an out. Turning her over would be the easy path.

But for all his bloodline, Tarian had an honorable streak a mile wide.

There were two choices. Option one was to react as she would if any other necromancer invaded her home. She was well within her rights to defend herself, as her instincts screamed at her to do.

Or she could choose a different path. See beyond his heritage to the man underneath and believe that the lover she'd pined for was still inside him.

She could choose to trust him, the way no vampire would ever trust one of his kind.

Swallowing hard, she took a step closer to him. "What would I do?" she asked, raising a hand to cradle his face. "I'd do exactly what you are doing."

He stiffened at her touch but didn't pull away. If anything, he seemed to lean into her hand. "Which is?"

"Turn to my lover for help."

Silence stretched between them. Tarian was doing exactly as she had just done—weighing the options, factoring in his feelings. All that remained to be seen was whether he'd choose her the way she had him.

"Are you so sure I'm not going to hand you over to Dominic?" he asked.

A smile curved her lips. "Yes," she replied. "I trust you."

His hands shot out to grab her upper arms and he tugged her closer. "My life would be a hell of a lot simpler if I didn't care about keeping you safe."

"Preaching to the choir," she replied.

A harsh curse left his lips before they crashed down on hers. Melissa didn't mind the rough handling. She could feel the desperation in his touch, taste it on his tongue. Tarian's back was up against the wall and this was the place he'd turned to. Even the direness of the situation couldn't stop the joy spreading through her body.

Melissa twined her arms around him, marveling at how she'd missed him. Over and over she'd told herself they'd just been a fling, that he wasn't her mate, but holding him now left little doubt about how important he was to her.

She couldn't imagine ever being over this particular man.

His lips slanted over hers as his hands slipped under the edge of her blouse. She groaned when his hands flattened against her bare back. Skin to skin contact was exactly what she'd been craving.

Tarian's mouth left hers to nuzzle the sensitive skin beneath her ear, and she tipped her head back to give him better access. Pleasure sizzled through every nerve ending, leaving her hot and aching. She wanted to jump into his arms and lock her legs around his waist. Wanted to fall into bed with him and block out the new disaster threatening to crash down on them.

But as much as her body cried out for fulfillment, she couldn't forget the girl Tarian had come here to save.

"Tell me you have a plan," she whispered, peppering his lips with kisses.

"A really bad one," he replied. "Part of me was hoping I'd get here and feel nothing for you."

"So much easier," she agreed. "Damned hormones."

He pulled back to look down into her face. "I think it's more than that."

Melissa bit back the smile threatening to curve her lips. "Yeah," she replied simply. "Tell me about this bad plan."

"I need your father's help."

She snorted. "You do remember when he banished you, right?"

"Maybe I'll grow on him."

"I think you might be his least favorite person, and he's met most of the villains in the history books."

"I don't need him to like me," Tarian replied. "But I need his help to trap Dominic."

"And I'm assuming your assistance in this matter won't come from the goodness of your heart."

A cunning smile flashed across his face. "Ironically, Dominic may have just given me the leverage I need to get Lucian to see reason."

"Where do I fit into this?" she asked.

"I need you to get him here so we can speak."

She stepped out of his arms. "I'll do my best, but keep in mind I'm a vampire, not a miracle worker." Grabbing the phone from its cradle, she punched in her father's cell number and waited for the call to connect.

On the fifth ring he picked up. "Melissa?" Lucian greeted.

"Are you in the city?" she asked, her eyes on Tarian.

There was a beat of silence before he replied, "There was a dispute I needed to mediate about an hour out. Why?"

"I need you to get back here as soon as possible. The situation with the necromancers has changed."

"How?" His voice was icy enough to make her shiver.

"The man who kidnapped me is in the city."

Tarian motioned for the phone and she handed it over. "Redgrave," he said. "I've been offered the chance to trade your daughter for my newly missing sister. You'll be happy to know it's not a deal I entertained, but the man behind Melissa's abduction doesn't know that. It appears I now have something to bargain with."

Melissa couldn't make out the words, but her father's tone was clear enough, and he was none too pleased with the turn of events.

"Just listen," Tarian said, cutting him off. "I am willing to meet with you to discuss the expansion of necromancer rights. In return, I will help you trap the leader of the dissenters. Fair trade, I believe."

He cocked his head, listening to something on the other end of the phone before nodding. "I'll be waiting for you at Melissa's apartment. Hurry."

He hung up before her father could reply.

"He is not going to be pleased with you," she said, catching the phone as he tossed it to her.

"I can't begin to tell you how much that bothers me."

Melissa rolled her eyes and returned the phone to its cradle. "So we've got some time."

"Yes."

"And there's nothing we can do right now to help Eilin?"

"No."

"Well then." She caught the hem of her blouse and tugged it over her head. "I believe you owe me some epic make up sex."

Fire leapt into his sapphire gaze. "I always knew you were a brilliant woman."

She sashayed backward toward the hall that led to her bedroom. "What do you think?" she mused. "Two orgasms to make up for your bad behavior?"

"Make it an even three," he replied, stalking her down the darkened hallway.

"I might not be the financial genius in the room, but even I know that's not an even number."

"Four should suffice then."

A grin curved her lips as her hand twisted behind her to catch the doorknob of her room.

"So many promises," she purred, undoing the zipper on her skirt. "I've been teased before."

His arm wrapped around her waist, hauling her against his chest. "Not this time," he vowed.

Her lips traced along his in a mockery of a kiss. "You left me," she whispered. "You walked away."

"I regretted every step," he replied.

"And when this is done and you've gotten what you wanted?" she asked, letting the skirt pool at her feet. "Will you walk away again?"

"No."

He met her gaze, offering no more assurances than that one word. Melissa knew she should rail till she was given a more encompassing promise, but he was right. These days vows were easy to make and hard to keep.

But it didn't matter. Being away from him had been hell. Pulling teeth was easier than trying to move on from the last man she should ever want. Being away from him simply hadn't worked for her. Now that he was back, she'd take him for however long they had.

At least she'd get an orgasm out of it. Or four.

"No more talking," she said, tugging his suit jacket down his arms. "I haven't decided if I believe anything you say."

"Then I'll have to prove myself with actions." True to his word he gripped his shirt and tugged. Buttons flew everywhere as his shirt parted like a costume on the set of *The Hulk*.

"I missed this," she murmured as her palms smoothed along his chest. She traced her fingers over his contoured muscles before ducking her head to run her tongue over the bronzed skin. He tasted like cinnamon and gold flecks. She nearly purred as she pulled one nipple into her mouth.

Tarian hissed under her caresses. Gripping her around the waist, he tossed her onto the bed.

She bounced once before his hands encircled her ankles and pulled her to the edge of the mattress.

"Someone's feeling a tad aggressive," she said.

"Impatient," he corrected.

"You're the one that left," she said, falling back onto the bedding. Twining her arms over her head, she arched her back. "We could have spent all week like this."

Daring a glance at Tarian, she saw molten lust in his eyes.

"I didn't have a choice," he said, crawling over her. "Doesn't mean I didn't miss you every minute. Is that what you wanted to hear?"

"Yes," she breathed, reaching one hand up to touch his cheek. "Tell me you're sorry."

"I haven't apologized to anyone in decades."

"If you want to get laid, you'll get over that rule," she said, reaching around her body to the clasp of her bra.

"Coercion," he argued as she stripped the straps down her arms.

"I have no idea what you mean." She let the bra drop over the side of the bed.

A grin flashed over his face as he ran his hands down her bare arms. "I'm sorry. I wish things had played out differently."

"That's much better," Melissa said, arching up to him.

"Vixen." His lips came down to claim hers in a fiery kiss.

Melissa closed her eyes and gave herself up to his touch. His lips teased hers, tasting, intoxicating. She wanted more, yet every time she parted her lips to deepen the kiss, he pulled back.

She moaned in frustration, her nails digging into his biceps.

"Did you miss me?" he whispered against her mouth.

Melissa groaned, falling back onto the comforter. "Turning the tables, hmm? My feelings for a decent kiss?"

"Yes," he said, tracing his mouth over hers.

Shivers ran down her spine as she returned the simple touch.

"I missed you," she acknowledged. "And dreamed of you. Every damned night."

His mouth pressed down on her in a dominating touch. Wrapping her arms around his back, she gave herself up to his expert touch. If Tarian was ready to get serious in their game, who was she to protest?

She clung to him as he drugged her body with endless kisses.

His hands wandered over her skin, pausing to caress and tease. Tarian pressed one thigh between hers and rubbed the rough material of his trousers against the sensitive silk covering her slit. She bit her lip as her thighs wrapped around his. Rocking her pelvis, she pressed her body against the enticing hardness.

"I need more than PG-13 touches," she said, undulating under him.

"Your wish," he murmured, undoing the zip of his slacks. "My command."

Melissa watched as he kicked free of his pants and tossed his boxers over her head in a triumphant show.

"One last thing," he said, hooking a finger around the edge of her black panties.

Melissa lifted her hips as he pulled them down her legs. The silk dropped from her ankle, but Tarian wasn't done. His burning hands pressed against her legs, tracing the smooth lines from ankle to knee.

"So beautiful," he breathed, leaning down to press his lips to the inside of her knee. He kissed his way up one thigh as his hand glided along the other.

Melissa threw back her head as she tried to hold her body still and wait until he reached the good parts. When his hot breath glided along her inner thigh she nearly arched from the bed.

"Tarian," she protested.

"I'm a man of my word," he said, one hand finding a

home on each thigh. Rolling his eyes up to meet hers, he pushed her legs apart.

The first lap of his tongue along her slit sent pleasure shooting through her extremities. As sensitive as she was right then, the slightest touch built her desire. His name rang inside her head as his mouth continued its sensual torture. He made a study of every fold of her anatomy before centering his attention on the small, tight nub of her clit.

"Tarian," she cried when he pulled the bulb into his mouth. Her hands cast out for purchase as she fought the need to drive her hands into his hair and push him closer. Instead she fought for control as he teased her with calculated touches. Every lap of his tongue sent her higher. Her body wound tight like a drum, waiting for the final touch that would release her.

"So close," she panted as he worked between her thighs. "Tarian, I want you."

She tried to pull him up, tried to communicate that she was on the edge, but he ignored every word. Instead, his grip tightened on her thighs and held her open as he plundered the most intimate parts of her.

"Yes," she breathed as her orgasm built. Just a little more. Another touch. Another lick.

His teeth scraped across her clit, and she screamed as her climax crashed down on her.

Pleasure swept her away. She bit her lip as her body spasmed. Every nerve ending exploded as she rode the sensations streaming through her body.

When the waves finally subsided, she fell back against the bed, satiated.

"Wow," she said.

"One," he replied. He pushed her legs open and nestled between them.

"You've got to give me a minute here," she said. "Mind blowing pleasure requires a moment of—"

He thrust into her.

"Cruel," she breathed as he sank into the deepest parts of her.

"We only have an hour," he replied. "And I need to make good on my promise."

Her eyes nearly crossed as she caught his meaning.

"I'm not sure that's possible."

His warm chuckle filled her ears. "Sweetheart, I promise you it is."

Gripping her hips, he slowly pulled out of her.

Melissa bit her lip as her sensitive nerve endings protested the renewed activity. She was almost ready to object when he sank back into her.

"Oh," she sighed, welcoming his long length. It was ridiculous how right everything felt when he was lodged within her.

Her teeth grazed against his shoulder as he increased his pace. She held on, raising her pelvis to every thrust. Together they writhed, racing toward a mutual satisfaction.

Tarian drove into her again and again. She closed her eyes and matched the movement of his body. True to his word, she felt the pressure building again within her. Melissa rocked to the rhythm, trying to satisfy that inner craving.

"Please," she panted.

"A little more," he breathed into her ear.

Closing her eyes, she gave herself up to the sensations he inspired. Pleasure rolled through her, inching her ever closer to another shattering climax.

She clutched onto Tarian and tried to hold herself back as he stroked into her, but with every movement it became a harder task.

"Soon," she whispered.

She never knew if he heard her. His cock drove deep, and she tightened her inner muscles, not wanting him to leave her again.

Tarian's guttural groan echoed in her ears.

As much as she enjoyed wringing such a sound from him, she couldn't last much longer.

He stroked back into her and Melissa released her death grip on her control.

Her orgasm crashed over her, more sweeping than the first. She felt Tarian pound into her, heard his heartfelt roar of release as he came within her.

Melissa barely paid any heed to the extra weight collapsing on top of her as her body gave in to the sensation racing through it. Pleasure coursed through her veins. She couldn't even form words to describe the experience.

When the aftermath subsided, she relaxed back into his arms.

"Two," he said.

She laughed. "Listen, Tarian, I appreciate the effort but consider the make up bill paid in full."

He wrapped his arms around her waist and rolled them so she straddled him.

"I don't think so," he replied. "I promised four and I never stop anything halfway through."

"Well," she breathed, looking down at him. "I've always enjoyed a challenge."

As he pulled her down for a kiss, Melissa wondered if she'd ever been as happy as she was that moment. And what did it mean that Tarian made her happier than anyone else in a hundred years?

"How much time do we have left?" Tarian asked.

Melissa couldn't even manage to turn her head to the clock. Her entire body was completely sated. Her lover had stayed true to his word and then some.

"Melissa?"

She groaned. "I'm betting not much."

"We should get ready."

"Says you. I'm not sure my legs still work."

Tarian rolled over her, propping himself up with his arms on either side of her head. She looked up into his face and marveled at the happy light in his eyes. She'd never seen him look so relaxed and carefree.

"What happens next?" she whispered, cupping his face.

"We brave your father," he replied with a roll of his eyes.

"No. I mean after. Say this plan of yours goes off without a hitch and Dominic is out of our lives forever. What happens then?"

Some of the joy in his eyes slid away. "What do you want to happen?"

She traced her fingers along the length of his jaw, avoiding his gaze. "I don't want this to be the last time I get to hold you."

"Then it won't be." He leaned down to press his lips to hers. Melissa closed her eyes and enjoyed the simple touch, meant to comfort, not arouse.

"Promise?" she whispered.

"I've been thinking I'm going to suspend my Fated

Match membership," he replied.

Her eyes snapped opened. "Why?"

"Because I met this woman, you see. And right now, I want to concentrate on her and not on securing a new date every week."

"I thought you were looking for your mate," she said. "Fated Match is the best way to do that."

"True," he agreed. "And in seven hundred plus years, joining that agency is still the best decision I've ever made."

"Oh?" She arched a brow.

"Because it introduced me to this incredible vampire. One I can imagine falling for so very easily."

Her heart clenched. She met his gaze and saw the sincerity in his eyes. "Me, too," she confessed. Those three little words were on the tip of her tongue, but she bit them back. It was too soon. They needed more time to get to know each other. Time away from the drama of disapproving parents and devious grandparents.

"Once this is over, we can figure out where we go next," he told her. "But for the record, I don't care where we end up, as long as you're in my arms every night."

"That sounds about right," she agreed, sliding her hands over his shoulders. Melissa pulled his mouth back down to hers and smiled against his lips. The next few hours would be some of the hardest of her life, but Tarian would be waiting for her at the end of it. They could figure out what they were to each other and, hopefully, spend days in bed.

Then she could see if the niggling suspicion in her brain was warranted. Despite the odds, Tarian might very well be her mate, and if that was the case, no power on heaven or earth would separate them again.

# Chapter Sixteen

The pounding on her door had Melissa sprinting to her entry wall.

"Ready?" she asked Tarian.

He shrugged. "As we'll ever be."

With a flip of the lock she pulled the door open.

Lucian barreled in like a storm. "Where is he?"

"Over here," Tarian said, lounging on her sofa. "Though let's all remember what happened last time you tried to attack me."

Her father bared his teeth. "Why are you still in the city?"

"The fact that you didn't know I was here tells me you have rather inept spies."

Abbey pushed into the room, forcing Lucian out of the doorway. "Hello, Melissa," she greeted. "We've got to stop meeting like this."

"Tarian has a plan to ensure that," she said, closing the door behind the pair. "Come on in."

"Who took my daughter and what are they doing in New York?" Lucian demanded, his eyes not leaving Tarian.

Her lover leaned forward, resting his elbows on his knees. "There is a small group of necromancers stirring the pot, and it's bad for all of us. They happen to be here in the city and it's our chance to catch them."

"You're doing this out of a desire to increase public safety and nothing more, I'm sure," Lucian drawled.

"No. I want equal rights for my people."

"Not happening."

"Then good luck finding this group." He leaned back on the sofa, utterly calm.

Abbey slid her hand up Lucian's arm. "What happens if we don't get this group?" she whispered into his ear. "More people will be in danger and this time, they might not have a guardian angel looking out for them."

"I've watched necromancers slaughter my people for generations."

"Lately?" Tarian asked. "Because we haven't even been allowed around your kind in a century."

"Listen to what he has to say," Melissa said. "It's not an unreasonable request."

Lucian's angry eyes turned to her. "I believe I ordered you to stay away from him."

"Going to ground me?" she replied, tapping her foot in impatience.

"Come on, honey," Abbey said, pulling Lucian into the living room. She guided him into an armchair and perched on the arm next to him. "Tarian, what are your terms?"

"I want necromancers allowed in all major cities. We will, of course, be held to the same standards as all other races.

No violence or threatening our cover with the humans. We just want the chance to live normal lives."

"Fair," Abbey said before Lucian could jump in. "And in return for this, you will give us the kidnappers."

"Yes."

"Who are they?" Lucian growled.

"Their leader is Dominic Salverg, my grandfather."

"Apple doesn't fall far from the tree," Lucian muttered.

Abbey whacked him over the head.

"You need a necromancer working with you to get close," Melissa said, moving next to Tarian. "Dominic will be on the lookout for vampires."

"I can set up the exchange. Tell him I have Melissa and will trade her for my sister. When I have the location, I'll relay it to you, and you can have your people standing by. I can handle my grandfather and you can corral the rest of his minions."

"Melissa is not getting anywhere near this."

Anger churned within her. She opened her mouth to defend her abilities, but Tarian beat her to it.

"Agreed," he said. "Besides, it's not necessary. We just need him to think an exchange is happening so he'll give us a location to trap him in."

She glared at her lover. While she appreciated the people she cared about trying to keep her safe, she wanted to contribute.

"It would help if you could call in the other elders," Abbey said, turning to Lucian. "Having backup that can't fall under a necromancer's spell would be helpful."

Lucian rubbed a hand down his face, but he didn't reject the plan out of hand. "The council is staying out of it," he replied slowly. "Without a formal declaration of war, they won't intercede."

"I have a few werewolf girlfriends I can call," Melissa offered. "Or Chloe at Fated Match might help."

"They'd get in trouble for going against their elders," Abbey said with a shake of her head. "Looks like we're on our own. How do we fight people who can stop us the moment they see us?"

Silence reigned.

*There's got to be a way,* she thought. *If we can't find a solution, Eilin will be in danger and Tarian will risk anything to save her. Even if he succeeds, he'll have to leave forever.*

And she was not willing to let him go. Not again.

"What if they can't see us?" she said.

Three sets of eyes turned to her.

"Dominic will want a location that is contained and private. If it's lit by electric lights, we can cut the power."

"Without our death magic we're practically human," Tarian said. "We're stronger and a bit faster, but we can't see in the dark the way vampires can. They'd never see their targets and without a visual link, their magic will be useless."

"Not a bad plan," Lucian said, "except that it will take time to hack into the electrical system. Will we know the location before Tarian arrives?"

Tarian shook his head. "Dominic will be careful. I probably won't know where he wants to meet until I'm about to walk into it. We won't have much forewarning."

"Which means we need time to tap into the system," Abbey murmured.

"We have to stall," Melissa said. "Keep Dominic occupied long enough for Lucian's guards to get in place and for the lights to die."

"He's going to know something isn't right as soon as I show up alone," Tarian said, running his hand through his hair.

"So you don't."

Again Melissa found herself the center of attention, and she lifted her chin. "If I go with you, Dominic will have no reason to believe you've switched sides. It will be the exchange he is expecting."

"No," Tarian said.

"Over my dead body," Lucian agreed.

She clenched her fists. "I'm all for the loving sentiments, but this is about more than one woman," she said. "Tarian has seen first hand that I'm not a helpless damsel in distress, and Lucian, you've taught me everything I know. I'm more than qualified to do this."

"I'm not risking my family to secure a few radicals. We'll go to war if need be."

"Really?" she demanded. "You're really going to put my life ahead of hundreds of vampires?"

Lucian looked away and triumph surged within her. She had him.

"A few minutes of my time and this will all be over with," she said. "Tarian will be there to help me, and you'll be following with the cavalry in minutes. What harm can I come to in that time?"

"You won't be immune," Tarian said, his eyes bleak. "If you do this, Melissa, you will have no protection from the necromancers around you."

She turned back to her lover, blocking out the room around them. "I know," she whispered, catching his hand in hers. "And I know protecting me can't be your priority. Too many lives depend on you springing this trap perfectly. If things go bad for me, I don't expect you to ride to my rescue."

"And if I can't help myself?" he asked, his voice rough.

Melissa closed her eyes and savored the moment. For once, she was the first thing on someone's mind. She wasn't the afterthought or the daughter. She was a person someone wanted to protect because he cared for her.

"Think of your sister," she whispered. "I know what I'm signing up for, and if things go south, I'll handle myself. My life is not on your conscience."

A hand wrapped around her neck, pulling her closer. "I can't compartmentalize like that," he said into her ear.

"You have to," she replied. "This is about more than you and me."

As gently as she could she pushed away from him and faced her father. "I've been your little girl for a century," she said. "But you need to let that idea of me go. I am choosing to do this out of my own free will. I understand the risks, and I believe the benefits are worth the danger. A lot of lives are riding on this, and you will not damn them merely because you can't conceive of a world where I don't need you."

"She's got a point," Abbey said, running her fingers through Lucian's hair. "You knew this day would come."

Lucian grit his teeth. "Loving your child isn't a switch you can turn off."

"But respecting her choices is a reality you can adapt to," Melissa replied. "I will go with Tarian and buy you the time you need to hack the electrical systems. Once you shut off the lights, I'll run for cover. Promise."

"They'll be armed," Lucian said.

"Then so will we," Melissa replied. "I've got some daggers here, and I'm sure you can supply suitable supplements if necessary."

"I'll have backup ready. If we can't kill the lights quickly enough, then we'll have to resort to the old-fashioned method and try to overwhelm them with numbers."

"I wouldn't advise it," Tarian said.

Lucian pinched the bridge of his nose. "The main goal has to be capturing Dominic. No matter what. I'll ensure all my guards know the risks."

"I just foresee one problem," Abbey said. "Say killing the lights works and you capture the necromancers in the dark. What happens when the lights turn back on?"

*They'll use their powers and force their guards to release them,* Melissa thought.

"We have to knock them out," Tarian said. "And once they're down for the count, we will need someone other than a death race member to take over their transport."

"I'll call the witches," Lucian said. "If we handle the violence, I'm sure the council will be willing to step in and transport the criminals."

"Well," Abbey said. "It sounds like we have a plan." She stood and grabbed her purse, rummaging through it as she moved toward Tarian. "There's just one more piece we need to discuss. Ah, here it is." She withdrew a gold folder and handed it over to Tarian. "I believe you'll be needing this."

"Abbey," Lucian said in warning.

Tarian flipped open the folder and picked up the first pamphlet inside, reading the title aloud. "'*So you're thinking about becoming an elder.*'"

"If this all goes according to plan and the necromancers

are welcomed into the supernatural fold, they'll need a voice on the council," Abbey said. "I got all the information from Miranda. Apparently the requirements are being at least six hundred years old, though older is preferred, and a leader of the community. That's usually determined by a vote, but under the circumstances, I think we can bend that rule a bit."

"You're championing his cause?" Lucian asked his mate.

She whirled to face him and crossed her arms. "Yes. From a human standpoint, the necromancer's banishment is ridiculous. Besides, this is an excellent idea and you know it."

"I could argue."

"You could," she agreed. "You could also spend the next two weeks sleeping on the couch."

"What do you think?" Melissa said, sliding up to her lover's side.

"Dos and don'ts of the council," Tarian read. "Do represent your race and support the unification of the supernatural community. Don't plot for world domination or commit crimes that can be easily traced back to you."

"Seems simple enough."

He closed the folder with a shake of his head. "This isn't a job for me."

"You are the only one fighting for your people," she replied with an arched brow. "Well, at least in a positive sort of way."

"I'm not a leader."

She snorted. "I beg to differ. And look at it this way. Half the council meetings are just people arguing with Lucian, and you're already really good at that."

A small smile touched his lips. "How about I promise to

think about it?"

"Fine," Lucian cut in. "Because if I don't get Dominic, you don't get the council."

"We'll get him. How long will it take you to organize your team?"

Lucian glanced at his watch. "We've got enough time before dawn. Give me twenty minutes then make the call."

"Tonight?" Melissa said. "We're not going to take a day to plan this out?"

Tarian shook his head. "I agree with Lucian. Dominic will be expecting me to act quickly, given Eilin is in his grasp. Prolonging the inevitable may raise his suspicions."

Abbey exhaled, puffing out her bangs. "Gotta say, this night definitely took a turn. I had dreams of getting to bed early and forcing Lucian to watch something dreadful on the reality TV network."

"Tomorrow, darling," he said, pressing his lips to her forehead.

Melissa reached out to link her fingers with Tarian's. "This will work," she said, more to herself than to him.

"It will," he promised, bending low to her ear. "And tomorrow we'll be free of all this."

It was a happy thought. Tomorrow would be the start of their fresh beginning.

All they had to do was survive the next few hours and take down the one necromancer strong enough to rival Tarian.

# Chapter Seventeen

The city lights flashed by the window as they sped downtown.

"You're sure about this?" Tarian asked again.

"Yes."

"Because we can come up with an alternative plan."

"We really can't," she said. "I'll be fine."

"Only if you're sure."

"I am."

"We could—"

"My God, I think I've changed my mind." She put her hand to her forehead. "I can't possibly take on this responsibility. Let me out so I can swoon on the street."

His lips twitched. "All right. I won't ask again."

Melissa reached out for his hand. "This will work. You and Lucian have been over every scenario. We've got Dominic's location, and my father's vampires are ready and waiting. All we have to do is talk until the lights go out, and if there's one thing I'm good at, it's charming, meaningless chatter. I tell you, my past as a socialite has prepared me for just this moment."

Tarian raised her hand to his lips. "I still don't like the idea of putting you in danger."

"We need this," she replied. "Besides, you'll be right beside me."

"Always."

Silence fell between them. Melissa tried to tell herself this was no big deal, but if she had a heartbeat, it'd be racing. Walking into Dominic's trap was like a rabbit skipping happily into a wolf's den.

But at least she had backup.

She studied Tarian's profile, bathed in the neon lights from beyond their window. He'd been rigid, his jaw clenched, since he'd made the call to his grandfather. Though she trusted him to do what was best for his people, she couldn't imagine the pain of betraying a family member. One who had been in his life for the better part of a millennium.

"You'll make an excellent elder." The words slipped out of her.

Tarian turned to her with shuttered eyes. "What?"

"I was just… When this is all over, you should take up Abbey's suggestion."

"It isn't a position I ever wanted to fill."

"I know but it's one you deserve. Everything you've done since we've met has been for the greater good. Your community needs a leader like that."

"For the greater good, or for a woman I found intoxicating?" he asked, turning back to the window.

She shook her head, even knowing he couldn't see her. "If the choice really came down to me or your people, I know what you'd pick," she whispered.

"Do you?" he replied. "That makes one of us."

Pleasure suffused her, but it didn't completely silence the nagging voice in the back of her mind.

"Will things change?" she asked.

"Change?"

"When you're an elder. I know it won't be the same as when we first met. You'll have to make decisions for thousands of people instead of just yourself. A vampire girlfriend might not be in your best interests."

For a moment he didn't move. When his head finally swung her way, Melissa found herself captured by the intensity of his gaze. He didn't twitch, didn't make any attempt to move closer, but still she felt the power of his presence pulse through the car. "I'm not going anywhere. Not until you ask me to leave," he said.

"Then you'll be here forever."

A ghost of a smile passed over his lips. "Good."

The car turned before she could say more. They drove into an underground parking complex, and tension filled her body.

"We're here," she said unnecessarily.

"Call your father."

She nodded, her phone already dialing.

"Here," Lucian said when he answered.

"We're arriving. How much time do you need?"

"We're surrounding the building, and my computer specialists are hacking the system, but it's more complicated than we suspected. We need at least fifteen minutes if not more."

She chewed her lip. Stall for fifteen minutes with an evil

genius who will want to throw a hood over her head and hustle her out immediately. Easy peasy.

"We'll do our best," she replied, and disconnected.

"Fifteen minutes," she said to Tarian.

"Damn," he said, no doubt echoing her concerns.

The car hit the lowest level of the structure and stopped.

"Remember to act scared," Tarian whispered as he reached for her.

"Not going to be hard."

He caught her chin and tilted her face up for a brief moment. "I'll never let anything hurt you."

"Back at you," she replied, closing the distance between them.

Their lips met and clung as if neither of them wanted to face the reality waiting beyond their doors.

*Mine,* she thought as she parted her mouth and flicked her tongue along his. They had to survive this night, because she was never letting Tarian go. Not to his grandfather and not to his position as elder. He was hers, whatever that meant. And she protected what was hers.

His fingers tightened on her jaw as he deepened the kiss. Fire flashed through her with the skilled glide of his lips. Closing her eyes, she gave herself up to the moment. Every inch of her wanted to pull him closer and forget about their mission. It'd be so easy to give up responsibility and go home to bed. She could have him naked under her, his head thrown back, his mouth gasping for fulfillment as she drove her fangs into his throat and drank.

With a groan she pushed him back against the tinted black windows. Her fingers curled into the soft material of his jacket as she kissed him with renewed desperation.

*Not the last time,* she tried to console herself. In fifteen minutes they'd be free. But the logic did not have the calming effect she'd hoped for.

She wanted to taste every inch of him, imprint his touch in her memory. She could live five centuries and never feel for another what Tarian made her feel with just a few well-placed caresses.

*I love you.* The words pressed against her lips but she bit them back. *No,* she scolded herself. *This isn't the time or place.*

"Let's go," she said instead, pulling back.

His dark eyes studied her but he made no comment. "Stay behind me," he said. "And leave the talking to me."

He opened the door, one hand moving to grip her arm.

*It's acting,* she reminded herself as he jerked her from the car. It was all a show for the man awaiting them in the center of the parking deck.

They left the car and started walking toward Dominic. Melissa gazed at the rows of parked cars and noted dark shapes keeping abreast of them. Looked like all Dominic's followers had decided to come tonight.

Despite the strong electric lights fighting back the gloom, the garage had a distinct menace to it. She reasoned it must have something to do with the looming threat of being kidnapped. Again.

"Grandfather." Tarian greeted him when they stopped a good ten feet away. "Where's Eilin?"

"Safe," Dominic replied, his eyes on her. "I see you managed to hold up your end of the bargain."

Melissa tugged at her arm for good measure and Tarian yanked her forward a few steps. "It was surprisingly easy."

"I would have thought those pesky morals of yours would get in the way."

"There is very little I won't do when it comes to my sister," Tarian replied, his voice cold enough to make her shiver. "Where is she?"

"You'll see her after our exchange."

"No," Tarian said. "I'll see her now or you will never get Melissa."

Silence stretched as the two necromancers tried to stare each other down. Melissa risked a glance at her lover and flinched at the icy look on his usually expressive face.

"Fine," Dominic spat. "You can have a look." He waved a hand and shadows from the edges of the lot moved.

Two necromancers dragged a struggling blonde into the light, and Melissa got her first look at the woman Tarian was determined to save.

Even knowing the girl was only a few decades younger than her, she still looked young. The regret in her eyes tore at Melissa's heart. She could only imagine being betrayed by blood.

"There," Dominic said. "All healthy and whole, just as promised."

"It was a mistake to take her," Tarian growled.

"We've been over this, dear boy. In a few years, I'm sure she will forgive the indiscretion."

"And me, Dominic? Do you think I'll forgive you?"

The older man sighed. "There is too much of your mother in you."

"My mother was the strongest woman I knew," Tarian snapped. "She kept me, and then Eilin, alive and out of your clutches."

"And think of how different your life would have been had she not. You fought for our cause once, Tarian, you could do it again."

"Never."

Dominic's empty eyes shifted to Melissa. "I don't know about that. With this act you'll be tarred with the same brush as the rest of us."

"I'm only doing what I need to in order to protect my family."

"What do you think about that, vampire?" Dominic said to her. "How do you like knowing your lover is ready to sell you out if the right offer comes along?"

"I think you can both go to hell," she hissed, hopefully convincingly.

"How ever did you catch her?" Dominic asked with narrowed eyes.

Tarian's grip on her arm tightened slightly before he opened his mouth. "It wasn't all that difficult. A little seduction and a few words of praise and she was eating out of my hand. It's not hard to get the better of a vampire desperate for a little attention."

This time there was no stopping her flinch and Dominic seemed to take vicious glee in her reaction.

*He's acting,* she reminded herself. *Don't pay attention to his words. You know you're more to him than that.*

"Yes, I've heard about Lucian's sheltered daughter. I imagine it wouldn't be very challenging to open her legs with just a bit of flattery and a show of interest."

*Don't kill him,* she repeated to herself in a running mantra. *Buy time.*

"Like I would ever stoop to considering a necromancer

as a viable partner," she said. "A girl can have a good time without envisioning white picket fences and starry futures."

"You should thank your lucky stars that one of us even deigned to notice you." Dominic sneered. "Tarian is much in demand."

She stiffened even as her lover drawled, "I can do better than the walking dead, Grandfather. She was fine for a single night but not an inventive enough lover to keep." His laugh sent spikes stabbing through her heart. Though she knew every word was an act calculated to buy Lucian the time he needed, she still couldn't help wondering if any of it was true. He hadn't fought for her when they came to New York. Not to mention, he was eons older than her. The old ones were notoriously hard to please in every aspect of their lives, especially the bedroom.

Had he been disappointed with her?

"Surely your spies told you I left her as quickly as I was able," Tarian continued, echoing her own fears. "I had no interest in the girl beyond some momentary pleasure."

Dominic's smile remained firmly fixed on his face. "My spies did relay that information. And the pain on the vampire's face seems to support your claim." He took a step closer. "But I also know you, Tarian. I find it hard to believe you'd sacrifice one innocent for another, even a disappointing lover."

Warning bells went off in her head. They weren't anywhere close to fifteen minutes and there was no denying the suspicion on Dominic's face.

"We've been over this," Tarian said. "As long as I get my sister back I'll do whatever you ask."

"So you say. But centuries of watching you indicates

otherwise." He snapped his fingers and Eilin was pulled back into the shadows. In her place a dozen necromancers appeared, forming an intimidating crowd down both sides of the parking garage.

"What is this?" Tarian demanded, looking around.

"Hand the vampire over," Dominic said. "If you do without protest, I'll give you Eilin and we can go our separate ways."

Melissa glanced around at the necromancers just waiting to take a piece out of her.

"Don't you trust me, Grandfather?" Tarian asked.

"No." A cold smile twisted Dominic's lips. "I don't."

She took a careful step away from Tarian in case she needed room to defend herself.

"Melissa, I'm sure you can see how this evening will end, and I'd rather not have to force you to come with me."

"You're asking me to meekly follow my kidnapper off to God knows where?" There was no hiding the disbelief in her voice.

"Yes."

"Go to hell."

"Such a shame."

The hairs on the back of her neck stood on end as she sensed Dominic's rising powers.

They were out of time.

• • •

She burst past him in a rush of speed. Tarian cursed as her slender hands wrapped around his grandfather's throat.

Chaos exploded around them. Necromancers rushed in

from all sides, and Tarian threw out his hands, unleashing his magic.

One of the guards turned and tripped another before running into one of the cement posts and knocking himself unconscious. Tarian immediate switched targets and took control of one of the men running toward Melissa. This one he ran into a comrade and grinned as they both went down.

But though his abilities gave him an edge, there were too many guards to stop all at one time. He was limited in what he could do, and the window where his powers were useful was quickly closing.

Melissa hissed at his grandfather as Dominic tossed her off him. She skidded a bit on the floor before launching herself back at her enemy, fangs bared.

Tarian waited for the inevitable moment where Dominic would freeze her in her steps, but the old man seemed to be enjoying himself. He twirled around Melissa, dodging her attacks and using his magic to nudge her blows just slightly off course.

He was a cat playing with a mouse, Tarian realized, and still Melissa didn't give up.

One necromancer reached him and he ducked under the wild punch. Rising behind the man, Tarian delivered a quick chop to the back of his neck before turning to face his next opponent. What he wouldn't give for his broadsword like in the old days.

Still, he'd never been a slouch when it came to hand-to-hand combat and he was centuries older than most of Dominic's followers.

He struck out in tight, calculated movements. Each attack found a vulnerable target, but no matter how many enemies he dropped, more swarmed in to fill their place.

A blow caught him on the side of the head and knocked him to his knees. With ears ringing he launched himself from the floor to strike out with hard fists. Through the fray of black uniforms he caught sight of Melissa standing perfectly still before Dominic. Looked like his grandfather had finally gotten tired of playing.

Kicking off the nearest guard, Tarian fought his way closer to Melissa. He didn't miss the triumphant smile Dominic shot his way before he turned to walk away, Melissa keeping pace at his side.

Dammit, where was that backup Lucian had promised? Fifteen minutes be damned, they needed help now.

As an answer to his prayers, vampires flashed from the stairwell. They barreled into the necromancers, working in pairs so if one was controlled the other could still fight.

The swarm around him thinned as Dominic's men turned to engage the new threat. Tarian saw bodies being thrown through the air and only hoped the vampires would make it until the power could be shut off. Some fought with lightning quick efficiency while others stood immobile before their captors.

Pushing himself from the ground, he looked around for Eilin and Melissa.

His sister was remarkably easy to find. She was fighting her guards, clawing at their faces, while a vampire team moved in to help her.

Knowing they'd get her to safety, he chased after Melissa.

Dominic hurried toward the farthest exit. He didn't even pause to see what had become of his supporters.

Pain throbbed in one knee as Tarian pushed himself

faster. He felt blood trickle from his temple but none of that slowed him. Melissa was still in danger.

"Grandfather," he shouted, stalking closer.

Dominic glanced behind and arched a brow. "You don't give up, I'll give you that."

"It's over. Surely you see that."

"I see no such thing. In fact, I think this is the perfect opportunity to get rid of you, Tarian. And I know exactly how to do it."

"I'm stronger than you in a fight," he said.

Dominic shrugged. "Who said anything about me fighting you?"

Melissa stepped up to his side, her eyes blank.

"No," Tarian breathed.

Dominic wasn't merely controlling her body, he'd taken over her mind. She stood before him as a puppet. Her vibrant personality had been deleted from existence. It was a defense only the strongest necromancers were capable of. Hell, he'd used this form of attack a time or two himself, but seeing it inflicted on someone he cared about sent rage surging through him.

"Melissa, darling," Dominic said, triumph shining on his face. "Do me a favor and destroy your lover won't you?"

Melissa flew at him without hesitation.

Tarian stumbled back. A necromancer's best defense against vampires was his magic. Without his powers, the odds were greatly tipped in Melissa's favor.

Claws shot from her fingertips as she hissed at him with glistening fangs.

"Melissa," he tried, even knowing it was useless. "Don't do this."

But there was no one home in her eyes. The influence she was under was deep and consuming. It reduced a captured vampire to little more than an animal. A perfect killing machine.

She leapt at him with raised claws.

Tarian spun around her attack, catching her foot to make her stumble. She righted herself with fluid grace and prowled toward him.

His mind whirled through his options while every instinct demanded he take down the threat. How many vampires had he killed in his lifetime? How many during the wars, who'd looked at him just like this?

A silver knife rested at his hip but he didn't draw it. No matter the situation, no matter how trapped Melissa was, he couldn't harm her. There had to be another way.

One clawed hand swiped at his chest and he blocked the blow with an arm. Choices, choices. How did both of them get out of this alive?

Teeth flashed passed his face, inches from his jugular, as he dodged his lover. He'd told her before that she was fierce when she wanted to be, and now he was seeing her abilities first hand.

She stalked around him, looking for a weakness. Every inch of her was a predator waiting to tear apart its prey. Each attack was blindly fast, her strikes razor sharp. Had he been watching her fight someone else he would have been awed at her grace.

As it was, he just wanted to stay a step ahead of her razor sharp nails.

Tarian blocked her strike and forced back the instincts that demanded he return the blow. He couldn't fight Melissa.

Which meant his powers were his only option.

*It might not be enough,* he calculated. Dominic was strong and his presence within Melissa would be hard, if not impossible, to dislodge.

Never before had he attempted to free a vampire of a necromancer's influence. He didn't know if he could do it now.

But if he couldn't, one of them was going to end up dead.

He waited for her next charge then grabbed her around the waist and tossed her to the floor. Tarian followed, rolling on top of her and pinning her hands above her head. Her jaws gnashed as she tried to reach his throat, mindless in her need to spill blood. He was running out of time. When it came to brute strength she had the edge.

"Look at me," he said, focusing his power on her.

Her struggles grew slower as he pumped his magic into her body. Never before had it been so hard to take over a vampire, but this time it wasn't the same as pouring magic into an empty vessel. Dominic's magic already filled her, fighting off his own.

His grandfather's laughter echoed over him, but Tarian never looked away from Melissa.

"Come on, sweetheart," he whispered, focusing on her blank green eyes. "Come back."

Prying Dominic's influence away was like trying to dry a flood with a Kleenex. Every time he got a foothold in her mind, Dominic was there to push him back out.

Her body bucked beneath his as he slipped again. With a snarl he dipped deeper into his magic. He fought to control not just Melissa but also the bastard pulling her strings. Deeper he delved, feeling Dominic's essence and chasing it down. Controlling a necromancer of Dominic's age and strength would be an impossible feat, but he refused to give up Melissa.

Deeper and deeper he went, calling on a well of magic he'd never touched before. Every fiber of his being was focused on one task. Failure was not an option.

Melissa stopped squirming under him. With every prolonged minute in her mind the process grew easier. Threads of his magic attached inside her body, chasing away Dominic's malevolence. Soon his power flooded her, seeping into every vein and cell.

With a groan he opened his eyes to gaze down at her.

"Come back," he whispered again. "Come back to me."

A heartbeat ticked by then another. On the third a miracle happened.

The woman he loved rushed back into her bright green eyes.

Melissa looked up at him, blinked, and then smiled the most beautiful smile he'd ever seen. In that moment, nothing else mattered but the fact that he'd gotten her back.

"Hello," he whispered, staring down at her.

"Tarian," she breathed. "I can feel you in my head."

"I broke my promise."

There was no accusation in her expression. "I forgive you. Stay in my mind. He won't be able to control me like this. I can fight with you."

His joy froze within him.

Choices, choices. Agree to her plan and she'd forgive him the use of his power, but she'd go back into the thick of things. Into a battle she might not survive.

He'd told her he respected her decisions, that he valued

her ability to fight and it was all true. But right now, with screams filling the air and Dominic's presence still prickling along his skin, he didn't want to put her skills to the test. He wanted her as far away from this as possible. There was no way he'd survive losing her twice.

And there was no way she'd move past such a betrayal. If he took away her choices, he'd have to watch her walk away from him. Permanently.

Which mattered more, her love or her life?

"Tarian," she said with a smile. "We've got work to do."

"No," he whispered, moving off of her. "Stand."

Melissa rose like a puppet on strings. "What are you doing?" she demanded.

He could feel her try to move her limbs as he held them still.

"Tarian," she said, panic entering her voice. "I'll never forgive you for this."

"I know," he replied. "Go to your father and do not look back."

Her eyes widened even as her body turned away from the fighting. "Don't do this," she cried as her legs started to carry her away.

Tarian didn't flinch. He poured enough magic into her body to ensure she followed his orders then turned back to the chaos in the parking lot. His chest throbbed like a physical wound. Even if he came out of this alive, she wouldn't absolve him for taking away her free will.

But at least she'd be alive to hate him.

He scanned the scene around him, looking for only one man.

*There.* Dominic was beating a hasty escape toward the

fire exit.

Tarian took off at a sprint just as the lights finally flickered.

Screams echoed off the concrete walls as half the parking lot plunged into blackness. Glancing over his shoulder, he saw the vampires swarming in, dragging their victims into the shadows to decrease their chances of being overtaken.

The main lights in his half of the garage flickered and went out, all except the emergency lighting over the exit.

Darkness gave vampires the edge, but there was still enough light for Tarian to track his quarry.

He increased his speed, pushing himself as fast as his injuries would allow. Cars flashed by him as he raced away from the chaos of the battle he'd left behind.

"Dominic," he shouted.

His grandfather whirled, glancing from him to the exit a short sprint away.

"You'll never make it," Tarian said. "Don't run away like a coward."

A growl rumbled from Dominic's lips. "I've fought more battles than you can count, boy."

Tarian slowed to a stop ten feet before his grandfather. "Then defeating me should be no problem," he said before launching himself forward.

Dominic met his attack, blocking each blow with a strength and speed only age could achieve.

Tarian tried to reach for the dagger on his hip only to have his legs kicked out from under him. He hit the ground hard, seeing stars as his skull cracked against the pavement. Dominic was on him before he could even roll over.

Hands latched around his throat and squeezed. A gasp

left him as his body struggled for air. His lungs burned as he fought the vicious hold.

Slamming his hands against his grandfather's elbows caused the older man's arms to buckle. Tarian gulped in air as he turned the tables. Wedging a leg between them, he kicked off Dominic and grabbed his blade.

He cast a leg astride his grandfather and stared down at one of the last remaining pieces of his family.

"Going to kill me?" Dominic said, looking at him and not the silver blade poised over his heart. "You know it's the only way you'll stop me."

He might be right. This man had caused wars and deaths across multiple continents for more years than Tarian wanted to think about.

But for all his evil, death was not the answer.

"I won't make you a martyr," he said. "This destruction ends with you."

"Our people will never stop fighting to be equal."

"They no longer have to," Tarian replied. "Dominic Salvage, as the newest member of the New York State Council of Elders, I am placing you under arrest."

Surprise shone in Dominic's eyes right before Tarian slammed the hilt of his blade against his grandfather's temple.

Dominic's body went limp beneath him, out cold.

Tarian rolled away from him and took a deep breath. He'd won. After all that, against all the odds, Dominic was finished.

He glanced back toward the other end of the lot. Though some necromancers still fought, the pile of unconscious bodies was growing. It would only be a matter of time before the battle was over.

As he rubbed a hand over his face, several vampires flashed to his side.

Staring up at their angry red eyes, he wondered if he'd be their next target, and tensed for a fight.

"Mr. Redgrave sent us," their leader said, pointing toward one of the security cameras he'd failed to notice. "He thought you might need a recovery team."

Tarian glanced at the camera. So Lucian had seen the whole thing and waited till it was over before sending help. Perhaps the elder had hoped Dominic would finish him off in the capture process. Tarian tipped his imaginary hat to the viewer on the other end of the camera before turning back to the vampires awaiting his orders. "Take Dominic into custody," he said. "Get him locked down before he comes to."

The vampires inclined their heads and grabbed Dominic's unconscious body. As they turned to go, the leader glanced back at him. "Mr. Redgrave says you have his thanks for protecting his daughter," he said. "Though he said to add, it won't do you much good when you see her."

"I didn't think it would," Tarian replied before waving them off.

The battle was all but won, and his people would soon be free.

He pushed to his feet, wincing as battered muscles stiffened in protest. There was still some cleanup to take care of and an angry vampire to face.

He hoped he'd made the right choice, because he had a feeling he'd be regretting it for eternity.

# Chapter Eighteen

Melissa stared up at the bright pink lettering above the glass doors.

*Fated Match,* she thought, *find your mate anytime, anywhere.*

Except it hadn't worked that way for her.

She'd ignored the texts and voice messages from this agency for two weeks. Though she was sure Abbey's heart was in the right place, she hadn't been up to rehashing the demise of her relationship.

If she closed her eyes, she could still see the regret etched on Tarian's face when he'd limped his way up to the control room. All her father's men had been busy securing and transporting the necromancer group. The witches had been standing by, ready to escort the trucks to the supernatural version of a maximum security prison. Last she'd heard, any death race guards employed at the prison had been transferred. There would be no chance of an escape using necromancer powers.

It should give her a sense of satisfaction, knowing Dominic would pay for his crimes, but all she felt was hollow.

Tarian had tried to apologize, tried to explain, but she hadn't wanted to hear it. Eventually he'd wrapped an arm around his shaken sister and walked out of her life.

Striding forward, she pushed open the glass door and stepped into the pristine waiting room of Fated Match.

"Melissa," Chloe called, rising from her seat at the reception desk.

She plastered a smile on her face and strode over to the witch. "You win. My voicemail gave up from exhaustion two days ago."

The other woman just grinned unapologetically. "I wanted to make sure you were okay. Abbey said you had a rough go of it."

"And then some," she agreed, leaning against the desk. "So they've got you manning phones?"

Chloe waved the question away. "I've seen four clients today, organized files, updated our systems and even managed a quick lunch. You know this place wouldn't run without me."

"Seems like it." Melissa glanced at the hall that led to the offices. "Is Abbey expecting me?"

"No," Chloe replied. "It's Vivian who wants to see you."

She arched a brow. What did the siren want?

Chloe shrugged. "You're a big client, and we kinda screwed you. You can't blame her for wanting to smooth any ruffled feathers."

"I don't have any," Melissa said. "It's not your fault I fell for the wrong guy."

"Still, let her grovel a bit. For me. Please?"

Pushing away from the counter, she inclined her head. "How can I refuse?"

Chloe clapped her hands and gestured down the hall. "She's free. Head on back."

Melissa turned away as the phone rang. Chloe give the standard Fated Match greeting as she headed down the hall.

Vivian had the largest office, hidden behind the last door in the hallway. She knocked twice before opening the door.

"Melissa," Vivian said, rising from her desk. "Come in."

She stepped into the elegant room decorated completely in silver. The white wallpaper was threaded through with silver stripes. Silver edged the colorless armchairs and coffee table.

Vivian's desk had the shine of metal even though it was designed like wood, and the gorgeous siren herself stood behind it.

"Please, have a seat," Vivian said, indicating the chair before the desk.

"I heard you wanted to see me," she said as she dropped into the chair.

"To apologize." Vivian took her seat and folded her hands over the gleaming desk. "As the head of Fated Match, I wanted to assure you we have taken your situation very seriously and made some changes around here."

"Oh?"

"It is no longer an option to refuse to disclose your race. We're looking into security measures for members and are thinking about offering a new service of monitoring first dates. From a safe distance, of course. Nothing obtrusive, but it will add an extra level of safety."

"For a price, I'm assuming."

The siren's smile never faltered. "In order to make reparations to you, I'd like to extend you our platinum level membership for the next decade. Free of charge."

"No offense, Vivian, but I'm not going to want to use your services for quite some time."

"I understand. We just wanted you to know how much we value your patronage and assist you in any way we can." Her smile slipped slightly. "Though the unfortunate events surrounding your abduction occurred outside of a Fated Match event, we still take responsibility for your chance meeting in our office."

"You also set up the first date."

"Yes. Our apologies."

Melissa shook her head. The siren would probably sell her to the necromancers herself if it brought in more business.

"I'd also like to make a personal recommendation of a were-cougar I know. Excellent fellow and no homicidal tendencies to speak of," Vivian said.

"Exactly what I look for in a man."

"Whenever you feel like getting back into the business of finding your mate, I'll be happy to make the introductions."

"And if I've already found my mate? What's your plan then?"

"I…" The siren's mouth opened and closed in shock. It would almost be comical if not for the tearing pain in her chest.

"I don't want another introduction," she said. "And I don't want the platinum membership. I'm done with the dating scene."

She had her charities and her friends. That was enough to fill a few lifetimes at least.

"I understand," Vivian said, recovering smoothly. "Please let me know if your opinion on the matter changes, and Fated Match will be there to assist you. Otherwise, thank you for your benefaction."

"Don't worry, Viv, I'm not going to torch your organization."

Some of the tension in Vivian's shoulders eased, though her pleasant expression never changed. "I assure you," Vivian said. "Our concern is for your well-being, not our reputation."

"Right." Melissa rose from her chair. "I trust you will stop flooding my phone with messages now?"

"Cross my heart."

"If you had one." The words were a cheap shot, but it didn't stop the slight tingle of pleasure when the siren's sharp nails left gouges in her shining desk.

Melissa stepped into the hall, shaking her head. Part of her admired the woman's entrepreneurial spirit. She was not one to let her business get tarnished without a fight.

"Did Vivian sink her claws into you or the other way around?" Abbey asked, leaning against the open door of her office.

Melissa paused, wondering how she could bypass the other woman without offending her. "Neither," she replied. "We had a civilized conversation."

"Better watch out, or she'll set you up on a date a night, just to bring you back into the fold."

"I think I can resist her lures." She started by Abbey only to stop when the human caught her arm.

"Lucian's worried about you."

"I'm fine."

"I'm worried about you. Hell, even Chloe's worried about you, and sometimes that woman is so damn cheerful you want to hold her down and tell her horrible things about the world."

"Time heals all wounds," she said. "And I'm immortal. I've got plenty of time to give."

"Have you talked to him?" Abbey asked.

She shook her head.

Her friend chewed her lip, as she often did when she was debating something. Melissa waited patiently for Abbey to speak.

"Lucian says he fit into the council nicely. They worked out a multi-step plan for phasing necromancers into cities around the country. I think their numbers within the city limits will still be capped and monitored, but it's a step in the right direction. He's a good choice to lead them."

"Good," she said, looking away from Abbey. "I'm glad it all worked out. His people deserve this chance." Glancing at her watch, she stared blindly at the tiny hands. "Look at the time. I've got to run, or I'll be late for an appointment."

"Then I won't keep you. Just…let me know when you want to get together."

"Drinks soon," she lied with a smile. "Tell Lucian I said hello."

"I will."

Melissa left Fated Match with a wave to Chloe as she passed by, and stepped out onto the street.

The moon was bright overhead as she made her way to her waiting car. Popping on her sunglasses, she ducked into the vehicle and gave instructions to run straight home. It was one of her rare days off and she had no intention of doing anything other than watching horrible TV and drinking a bottle of wine. Or two.

As the city glowed beyond her window, she let her forehead fall against the glass. Abbey had meant well, but she didn't want to talk about Tarian. The tearing in her chest hurt too much.

Logically, she understood he'd made a decision he thought was in her best interest. Hell, even Lucian had thanked him for sending her out of the fighting. But Melissa didn't know if she could forgive his choice. Had he always thought she was weak? That she couldn't defend herself? When had she ever given that impression?

But even if she could get over his lack of faith in her abilities, she couldn't get over the icy grip of his magic.

His power had run through her veins, robbing her of any free will. Dominic had enspelled her mind, but Tarian had commanded her body. The magic she'd once thought of as familiar had taken her over, proving to be more alien and desolate than she'd ever imagined. That, more than anything, was the reason she couldn't see him. She was not a woman afraid of much, but when it came to Tarian's abilities, every hair on her nape stood on end.

And what sort of relationship could she have when she was always on guard, waiting to see if her lover would snap his fingers and take away her free will?

It would never work. It should never have been started in the first place. Their romance had been idealistic and naive right from the beginning. Tarian couldn't cut off a part of himself, and she wasn't in the business of trying to change people even if he were willing. His magic was as vital to him as her fangs were to her. With another woman it wouldn't be a problem, and he deserved the chance to find that happiness. Even if it wasn't with her.

She opened her eyes to look out at the street.

Was it possible for him to be her mate but her not to be his? She'd dealt with breakups before. Ones that had lasted decades instead of days. And yet never before had she felt so empty inside. Like a part of her was missing.

It wasn't fair that this city was filled with happy matches and hers had been doomed to failure right from the start.

She had no idea how she'd react when she saw him again. And their paths would cross. The council was a staple on her invite list for all her balls and galas. Tarian would come with the rest to represent his race. She'd have to shake his hand and smile, all the while pretending she didn't miss him with every fiber of her being.

"We're here, miss. Would you like me to see you up?"

"No need," she said to her new driver. "I'll be fine." It wasn't like she was a target any longer.

Melissa exited the car and made her way into her apartment building. The werewolf doorman bowed as she walked by, but she didn't feel like stopping for a chat, as she would have most nights. Instead, she crossed the marble entrance-way and made a beeline for the elevators.

Maybe she should travel, she mused as she pressed the button for her floor. It'd been ages since she'd last been to Europe. She could take a few weeks and wander the streets she'd known in decades past. Looking up old friends might get her mind off of Tarian.

The bell dinged to indicate her floor, and she stepped

from the elevator, planning her vacation as she did so.

Melissa was so preoccupied she didn't notice the figure by her door until she had nearly reached it.

When the man turned to face her, her stomach dropped to her toes.

"Melissa," Tarian said.

# Chapter Nineteen

Seconds ticked past as her mind whirled with her options. Turning and walking the other way seemed a good choice, but that would be the coward's way out. She could ignore him and simply enter her apartment but that also seemed rather childish. The adult thing to do would be to smile and make small talk, pretend his presence didn't make her bleed. However, seeing him there, looking every inch as gorgeous as she remembered, she didn't know if she could pull off "unaffected."

"Tarian," she greeted him, lifting her chin. "I was not expecting you. If you require an appointment to discuss council business you can make one with my secretary and meet me at my office between the hours of ten and three."

A tiny smile twisted his lips. "This isn't about the council, and you know it."

"Then we have nothing to discuss." She strode to her door and unlocked it, trying to ignore the prickling awareness on the back of her neck, which had never been there before. She didn't want to fear him, but her instincts screamed to get away from the necromancer as soon as possible.

"Going to invite me in?" he asked, leaning against her doorjamb.

"You didn't need an invite last time."

"That was different."

She glanced at the door, not wanting to look into those eyes she'd fallen in love with. "I don't have anything to say to you."

"I know," he breathed. "But I have things to say to you. Please, Melissa. Let me in."

She wavered. Despite the logic telling her anyone with his abilities should be avoided at all costs, her heart still clenched at the sight of him. Maybe this would help. She'd hear him out and then they'd have closure. They could meet as polite strangers next time.

"Fine," she said, stalking into her apartment. "You have five minutes."

She kicked off her heels as Tarian closed the door behind them. Ignoring him, she went to the kitchen and pulled out a bag of blood.

He waited in silence as she poured the red liquid into a novelty mug Chloe had given her that read "got blood?" on the side and popped it into the microwave.

"Your time is ticking," she reminded him, watching her mug rotate on the glass plate.

"Look at me."

The microwave beeped, and she pulled out her drink.

"I don't need to," she said as she turned, blowing on her mug. "I know what you look like." She tried to stalk past him but he caught her arm.

Taking the cup from her fingers, he set it on her floating island before tipping her chin up.

The blue of his gaze filled her view. For a brief instant, all she wanted to do was wrap her arms around him and block out the rest of the world. When he held her, all their problems fell away. They could go back to being the partners they'd been on the road. The ones learning to trust, too naive to believe the other would ever break their word.

He drew his knuckles gently over her skin. "God, I've missed you," he whispered.

She closed her eyes and tried her hardest not to melt beneath his touch. "This isn't helping either of us," she said. "You should leave."

"I will if you answer one question."

She looked back up at him. "What?"

"Do you love me?"

Her already battered heart shattered. They were not going to do this. She would not stand here and rehash everything that had gone wrong. She couldn't bear it. To hell with closure, she wanted him gone before she revealed even more pitiable secrets.

"Leave," she said, her voice flat.

"You know how to get rid of me," he replied, one thumb brushing against her lower lip. "Tell me you don't love me, and I'll never bother you again."

"Did you forget what led to this lovely moment we're having?"

He shook his head. "I don't deny there are complications with our union, but I believe the benefits far outweigh any potential risks."

"Going to woo me with finance speak?" she taunted.

"I'm trying to tell you every day I spend away from you is hell."

She looked down. It should be comforting to know she wasn't suffering alone, but instead it just made her sad that he was living the same pain she was.

"We can't change what we are," she whispered. "It makes no difference if I love you or not."

"It does," he replied. "I've waited centuries to find the one woman I'd spend eternity with, and I knew the first moment I saw you, Melissa. You were the one for me."

She dragged her gaze back to his. "You said I wasn't your mate."

"I lied."

The vise on her heart tightened even more. "I can't be with someone who thinks I'm weak and in need of protection."

"You are, without a doubt, a dangerous adversary, sweetheart," he replied. "You fought me, remember? Every movement was elegant, lethal, and anything but weak."

"You sent me away like a child."

"Know why?"

She rolled her eyes. "For my own good."

"No," Tarian shook his head. "For mine. The thought of a world without you in it destroys me." He stared down at her, every line of his face etched with sincerity. "I was trying to protect you because my world stops if you get hurt. It wasn't a comment on your skills. If anything, it shone a spotlight on my weakness, not yours."

She snorted. "You have a weakness?"

His hands cupped her face. "When it comes to you I do. I will always try to protect you, Melissa. It's not an instinct I can shut off. That's what happens when you find your mate."

Ripping herself away from the comfort of his touch, she paced over to her living room. She looked out the tall patio windows as she wrapped her arms around herself.

"It's not just that you didn't trust me to fight," she said.

"I know." The words were soft from behind her.

She saw his reflection in the glass as he stood behind her right shoulder. "I can't be with someone I can't trust. Your powers are just too strong, Tarian."

Hands skimmed over her shoulders in a light touch. "I could vow to you I'd never make this mistake again, but to be honest, I don't know if that's a promise I can keep. If I ever saw you in danger again, my instincts would be to save you any way I could."

Pain slashed through her. Part of her had actually hoped for promises, false or not. Then she would have had an opening, a way of thinking seriously about their future. She could have fooled herself into believing it had only been one slip. That it would never happen again, and she could love him the way that she craved.

But instead he gave her honesty. She should appreciate the gesture instead of damning his integrity.

"Then there is no solution," she said.

A tiny tinkling reached her ear, and she saw something shine in the window reflection.

Turning, she saw the rield bracelet dangling from Tarian's fingertips.

"I thought you couldn't make another," she breathed, staring at the answer to all their prayers.

"I can't," he agreed. "But I was able to secure this one from Dominic before he was tossed into prison." He wound the silver strand around his fingers. "You know how powerful these pieces are. He wasn't about to throw it away."

She reached for it, but he pulled his hand back. "No," he said. "I'll not give it away so easily twice."

Melissa frowned, wondering what new game they were playing.

"The first time I gave you this bracelet I was filled with noble intentions. I thought myself to be an upstanding, moral man who would never stoop to manipulating a lover, no matter how dire the circumstances. I gave you this rield as a way to convince you I could be trusted, not because I thought it would ever matter that you wore it."

"And now?"

He studied the silver twining around his fingers. "Now I know giving this bracelet away restricts my options. I might have to watch you get hurt one day. Hell, I might have to watch you die, knowing that if I hadn't given you this rield, I could have saved you."

"Every couple fears losing each other," she whispered.

"You took a few decades off my life when Dominic had you under his power," Tarian said. "I never want to feel that way again."

"I can protect myself," she replied. "And what's more, you can be around to be my backup."

He inclined his head, playing with the rield. "There's another piece to consider. You nearly killed me when we fought. Without my magic I'll be at your mercy."

She bit back the smile that threatened. "I might be stronger," she pointed out. "But you also weren't really fighting me. Dominic might have been pulling the strings but I still remember every moment of that night. You only defended yourself, Tarian. You did everything in your power to avoid hurting me."

"Always," he breathed, taking a step closer.

"What if I promise to be gentle with you?" She rose to her tiptoes. One hand pressed against his chest to steady herself as her lips nearly brushed his.

"Trust," he whispered against her lips. "This all comes down to trust."

Melissa drew back slightly, meeting his gaze. Trust. She had to trust him not to abuse his powers, and he had to trust her not to take advantage of her immunity with the rield. It was a risk for them both.

Cool metal touched her wrist and she looked down to see Tarian clasping the bracelet over her hand.

"I love you," he said.

A shudder ran through her. As often as she'd prayed to hear those words, nothing could compare to the reality.

"Be my mate," Tarian whispered in her ear as he pressed a kiss to the sensitive skin. "Mine for all eternity."

Tipping her head back, she closed her eyes. His lips trailed down her throat in a gossamer caress.

A startled cry escaped her when he caught her around the waist and twirled her backward toward her high-backed beige couch.

"I don't care if you won't give me the words," he said, pressing her down onto the sofa as he watched her with burning eyes. "I don't care if it takes me centuries to pry them from you. I know you love me."

"Centuries, hmm?" She traced her fingers along his jaw.

He caught her fingers and pressed them to his mouth. "Though I do hope it won't take quite that long."

She smiled. "Are you so sure I love you, Tarian?"

"Yes."

"Tell me why."

He pressed another kiss to her fingertips before drawing her up into a sitting position. "Do you know when Abbey told me you were missing, I experienced a panic I haven't felt since I was a young man?"

She arched a brow. "What does that have to do with me loving you?"

"Nothing. But it has everything to do with me loving you," he replied. "I knew then you were important to me. And on the road when you could have run but came back to see if a child needed help, that's when I knew I wouldn't be able to forget you." He turned her palm over and pressed his lips to the tender skin. "But it was when you stood up to your father in order to fight beside me that I knew I'd love you until the end of my days." Tarian cupped her face between his palms. "How could I travel on this adventure with you, Melissa, and fall for you so completely, without you feeling anything in return?"

"Surely the universe isn't so cruel," she teased softly.

A smile curved his lips. "You love me. Whether you admit it or not."

She reached out to press her hand above his heart. The sturdy thump beneath her fingers steadied her.

"I wanted to hate you when you showed up at Dominic's ranch," she said. "And then you insisted I stay with you, and all I wanted to do was escape."

"I know." He leaned closer, his lips brushing against her cheek.

"Then you changed everything," she whispered. "I was

never supposed to care for you, but I couldn't help myself."

"I understand completely." His lips brushed against hers.

"You're the last man I should love."

"I'm not arguing."

"So then why can't I stop?"

He drew back to meet her gaze. "Because we're meant to be."

"I love you." The words burst from her, no longer able to be contained.

Pleasure lit his face. "Again," he demanded.

"I love you." The second time was easier than the first. Wrapping her arms around his shoulders, she cast a leg astride his thigh and shifted into his lap. "I loved you even when I didn't want to."

"At least we're caught together." His hands rose to her hips to stabilize her.

"This won't be easy," she said. "With your position, and my father…"

"Don't you see, sweetheart? None of that matters. Not anymore. No one can separate mates."

"Promise?"

"Forever."

His lips claimed hers as she gave herself up to the pleasure of his touch. Everything was different now. He was hers. For eternity. Her mate.

She smiled against his mouth, unable to contain her joy.

"I'm going to have to apologize to Vivian," she breathed, tilting her head back when he scraped his teeth against her neck.

"No doubt she'll put us on posters as one of her success stories."

"Fated Match. Find your mate anytime, anywhere," she quoted.

"Even the most unsuitable ones."

"In the most unusual circumstances." She drove her fingers into his hair. "I don't know what I would have done had you not walked into that agency."

"Somehow we would have found each other." Conviction burned bright in his gaze. "One way or another, you were always my destiny."

He tumbled her back down onto the couch, not that she had any complaints.

Gazing up at her mate, she knew he was exactly right. No matter how many times the universe had screwed her in the past, bringing Tarian into her life more than made up for it.

"I love you," she said, pulling him down to her. "Forever."

He smiled as he kissed her, his touch promising what she already knew. After all her wrong turns, her luck had finally changed. Fate had given her the man of her dreams, and she didn't intend on ever letting him go.

# About the Author

Victoria Davies's love for writing started young. Luckily she had a family who encouraged believing in magic and embracing imagination. From stories quickly scribbled in bright pink diaries, her love of storytelling developed. Since then her characters may have evolved and her plots may have grown decidedly more steamy but she never lost her love of the written word. Writing is not only a way to silence the wonderful voices in her head, but it also allows her to share her passions with her readers.